"Don't touch me, Gray," Donna begged as his finger caressed her ear.

He removed his hand unhurriedly, his thumb "accidentally" trailing across her upper arm. "Sorry," he said. "Don't you like to be touched?"

"I . . . Yes, but . . ."

"But what?" There was a gentleness in his voice, in his eyes, that made her feel all dreamy and unreal, made her ache for the touch she'd told him she didn't want.

"But—but I don't know you," she managed to say.

"And isn't that why we're together, to get better acquainted? What better way to get to know each other than my . . . touching you?" He stroked a hand from her shoulder to her wrist. "And your touching me? While we talk."

He took her hand and placed it on his chest halfway up, partly on his shirt and partly on his bare skin. Her fingers, as if with a will of their own, slid off his shirt and pressed over the hard beating of his heart.

"When I kissed you after dinner, your lips answered mine. . . ."

WHAT ARE *LOVESWEPT* ROMANCES?

They are stories of true romance and touching emotion. We believe those two very important ingredients are constants in our highly sensual and very believable stories in the *LOVESWEPT* line. Our goal is to give you, the reader, stories of consistently high quality that may sometimes make you laugh, sometimes make you cry, but are always fresh and creative and contain many delightful surprises within their pages.

Most romance fans read an enormous number of books. Those they truly love, they keep. Others may be traded with friends and soon forgotten. We hope that each *LOVESWEPT* romance will be a treasure—a "keeper." We will always try to publish

LOVE STORIES YOU'LL NEVER FORGET
BY AUTHORS YOU'LL ALWAYS REMEMBER

The Editors

549

Judy Gill
Summer Lover

BANTAM BOOKS
NEW YORK · TORONTO · LONDON · SYDNEY · AUCKLAND

SUMMER LOVER

A Bantam Book / June 1992

If you would be interested in receiving protective vinyl
covers for your Loveswept books, please write to this address
for information:

Loveswept
Bantam Books
P.O. Box 985
Hicksville, NY 11802

ISBN 0-553-44259-7

Published simultaneously in the United States and Canada

PRINTED IN THE UNITED STATES OF AMERICA

OPM   0 9 8 7 6 5 4 3 2 1

Summer Lover

One

Donna Mailer paused in the doorway of the large, sun-filled office, gazing with unconcealed curiosity—and not a little well-hidden apprehension—at the man who rose swiftly to his feet behind a desk piled with paperwork. He returned her stare, obviously making his own assessment, and just as obviously liking what he saw.

He smiled. It began in his eyes and then creased his face, parting firm looking lips and revealing a crooked canine tooth, then letting a dimple flash in his right cheek. The sun shot blue lights off his dark hair. He was so different from what she'd expected, and so different from what his brother Jamie had been, that she felt abruptly out of her depth. He wasn't classically handsome, but something compelling about his looks, his silvery-gray eyes, almost forced her to stare.

"Ms. Mailer," he said, his voice rich and warm and rumbly. "I'm Gray Kincaid. It was good of you to come."

Gray? She'd only heard him called Graham. The short form of his name suited him, she thought,

especially because of those eyes. "Mr. Kincaid."
She struggled to keep her voice cool, and let it
come out all breathless and feminine, the way his
smile made her feel. She was not there to let this
man bamboozle her with a gorgeous smile and
gorgeous hair and an admittedly great physique.
He was a Kincaid, dammit, and she'd been bowled
over by them once already in her life. Never again.
Jamie Kincaid and his father Chester had done
enough to her. The half brother wasn't going to get
even half a chance.

She was there to listen to his newest offer for her
uncle's campground. In all likelihood, she would
then turn on her heel and march out. She didn't
like having to deal with a Kincaid, and would do it
only because Uncle Tyler had insisted that maybe
this offer, coming not from Chester but from his
son, might be better than the last one. She was
sure it would not be, but she'd listen. And likely
refuse. With utmost pleasure. Five minutes, tops,
and she'd be out of there.

She drew a deep breath and let the door swing
shut behind her.

"Come and sit down," he said, his voice so
warm, she could have wrapped herself in it and
toured the arctic. He stepped out from behind the
desk, his long, loose-limbed stride bringing him
across the room to her before she'd taken more
than two steps on the thick cream-colored carpet.
He wore a summer-weight suit the same shade of
gray as his eyes, a dazzlingly white shirt, and a red
tie. He looked, she was forced to admit, far more
attractive than she'd ever anticipated.

Where were the horns? What had happened to
the spiked tail? Why wasn't he wearing a red suit
and breathing fire? And why had Jamie painted
him in such lurid colors?

"It's good to meet you, Ms. Mailer. Or may I call you Donna? I hope you'll call me Gray."

He extended a hand, which she took, surprised to discover hard calluses on his palm. Jamie's hands had been softer than hers. She doubted that even at the age of twenty this man would have had soft, doughy hands like his brother. Only then, she'd thought of Jamie's hands as "gentle." The term "doughy" had never occurred to her until that very minute. The thought raised a vague kind of guilt.

"You can't imagine how amazed I was," Gray went on, "when your uncle told me that if we wanted to make another offer for Clearwater Camping, we'd have to make it to you." His grip was as warm as his voice. To her shock, it sent a tingling sensation of electricity up her arm, arrowing straight to several sensitive zones on her body. She was certain he would see two in particular through the silk of her blouse if he glanced down.

He glanced down. When he looked back up, he met her gaze with a slow smile, half-playful, half-rueful, acknowledging what they both knew, acknowledging that whatever she felt, he felt too.

Quickly, she took her hand back.

"For one thing," he continued, resolutely keeping his gaze on her face now, "I didn't even know Tyler and Sadie had a niece."

"I've been living in the Maritimes."

"So Tyler said. And that you haven't had much contact with them for almost ten years." He took her arm and drew her, not toward the desk and the oak visitor's chair in front of it, but toward a deeply cushioned sofa under the corner windows. "The Maritimes' loss is definitely British Columbia's gain."

He seated her, then sat half facing her, hitching

up the knees of his sharply pressed pants. He cocked his head to one side, assessing her again, his eyes full of friendly warmth. "If I hadn't known you were related to someone I know, I'd have still thought you looked familiar." His smile was faintly quizzical. "But for the life of me, I can't decide if it's Sadie or Tyler. I suppose it has to be one of them, since they're the only relatives of yours I've met."

"They are my only living relatives, and I don't think I resemble either one," she said. "Though if I do, it must be Uncle Tyler. My mother was his younger sister."

He laughed. "Tyler, if you'll forgive my saying so, looks like a basset hound."

He grinned and she found herself responding, laughing breathlessly. He was absolutely right. Uncle Ty did look like a sad old hound dog.

Gray liked Donna's smile. He liked her light laugh, too, liked it a lot. He liked her silky hair, its color midway between red and brown—chestnut, he guessed—pulled back from her heart-shaped face with what his daughter called a banana clip. But it was her smile that drew him. That was where the resemblance lay, there and in her big, deep brown eyes. Tyler's eyes, he remembered from his visit to the nursing home, were a faded, tired blue. He shook his head.

"No way," he said. "Not even when you're old and gray and stooped, are you going to look anything like a basset hound." He stared into her eyes for much too long, then his gaze swept down her face to her shoulders, and rested for a moment on the erotic hint of satin and lace bra cups beneath the peach-colored silk of her blouse.

Completely unable to control the impulse, he reached out and touched her hair, lifting a lock of it and letting it slide through his fingers. "I like your hair," he said. As the lock he'd touched slid back against her neck, she shivered, as if he'd caressed her. He saw and heard her draw in a sharp breath, and a quick peek showed him that her nipples had leaped into the same kind of response as his last touch had elicited.

He didn't smile this time, but shifted as his body hardened uncomfortably. His gaze on hers, he read in her eyes the same kind of confusion and half-hidden excitement he felt pumping through his own veins.

She bit her lip and he wanted to kiss it. It was only fair, he told himself, that she should suffer the same kind of discomfort as he did whenever he so much as looked at her.

Donna felt her breasts swell and struggled to get a tight grip on her emotions. It was nearly impossible, though, with his intense gaze locked on hers, silently acknowledging that something sexual was definitely going on between them. Dammit, they were strangers! She did not, ever, respond this way to a man she didn't know and trust. Or she hadn't, until today.

After a moment, during which she tried to draw in a breath, Gray sighed softly. With obvious reluctance he turned his attention to the coffee table before the couch and lifted an insulated pot, which had clearly been there waiting for her to arrive.

"Coffee?" he asked. "I could have some Danish or muffins brought in, but it's nearly noon and I'm hoping if you get hungry enough, you'll join me for lunch after we've talked business."

She gulped against the dryness in her mouth and throat. "Lunch?"

"Yes. That meal people normally enjoy in the

middle of the day. I'd enjoy mine a lot more if I had you across the table from me, Donna."

Lord! Those eyes! The messages they were sending! And she wanted, suddenly and very badly, to agree.

"No!" It came out much too forcefully. For an instant, she thought he looked hurt by her abrupt refusal, and almost regretted it. "No," she said again, less sharply. She tempered it more by adding, "Thank you. Not lunch."

He shrugged one shoulder. "Coffee, then?"

Donna considered. This was not the way she was accustomed to conducting business, but maybe things were different out here on the supposedly laid-back Pacific Coast. Besides, what harm could it do to share a cup of coffee with the man?

She drew herself up short. What harm? Where were her brains? He was a Kincaid. She shouldn't have to ask what harm. She knew what harm. Look at the harm done her by a childhood friendship with another Kincaid, a friendship that had turned into tender, gentle first love, then was followed by a terrible betrayal, destroyed by the power and wealth of this man's father. Not that a cup of coffee constituted friendship, and not that she was an innocent sixteen-year-old anymore, but the principle was the same. This man was Chester Kincaid's son, and Chester Kincaid was her enemy. She was supposed to be on the alert here, not responding physically to the guy and getting all silly and inane over the sound of his voice, the touch of his hands, the gleam in his silver-gray eyes. . . .

She pulled herself up short with a quick reminder that Chester had been trying for years to lever her uncle's campground off Cordoba Island. Since he'd lost every legal battle he'd ever instituted against Uncle Tyler, he'd obviously thought that now Tyler was old and forced into retirement, he could shut the place down by buying it—for a price well below market value. When that had failed, had he deliberately sent his son into the fray, with orders to mesmerize Donna Mailer, who was a proven easy lay?

Sitting straighter, wishing for the hard chair opposite Graham Kincaid's desk rather than this soft leather couch, she glanced at her watch and said, "I have a lot to do today, Mr. Kincaid. Shall we get down to business?"

He smiled, mockingly she thought, as if he were secretly laughing at her, as if he knew how hard it was for her to keep from surrendering to his charm. "Business? Certainly, if you insist. But I always find business moves a lot more smoothly if people try to meet each other on a friendly footing." He filled the cup nearest himself, and the aroma of coffee tantalized her. With one brow arched, he angled the spout over the second cup.

"Will you have some?"

She hesitated another moment, thinking how ungraciously she was acting. He was right. There was no reason why they couldn't conduct their business in a friendly manner. The caffeine might help to sharpen her instincts, keep her alert when she was tempted to let herself be carried into dreams by a certain light in those damned gray eyes of his. Sweeping her gaze over his craggy face, noting his square chin and sharp, intelligent eyes, she thought she'd be well advised to keep her mind as finely honed as possible in dealing with this man.

Five minutes and out, she reminded herself.

"No coffee, thank you," she said. "I believe your company has an offer to make? I understand from my uncle that you claim it's better than the original one." Her tone indicated serious doubts.

With a sigh and another of those faintly mocking smiles, he nodded and rose lithely to his feet. He strode to his desk and returned with a file folder. Sitting beside her again, he tapped the edge of the folder on his thumbnail.

"I agree," he began, "that the offer my father made in April was somewhat below the assessed value for the land. But it did reflect the market conditions that were prevalent at the time, as well as the condition of the business."

"Land values fluctuate," Donna conceded, "but the market appears to have bottomed out and is now on the rise again." For the past week she'd been studying the back issues of every real estate publication in the area. Chester Kincaid's first offer had been an insult.

"That may be true," Gray said, "but there is still very little market for such a large parcel of land as you're offering."

"We aren't simply offering a large parcel of undeveloped land. You seem to be forgetting that what we have is a long-established business that enjoys considerable goodwill. The returns on an investment of that nature are excellent. We believe your previous offer failed to reflect that."

He cocked one eyebrow. "According to our figures, the returns on the investment would be less than 'excellent,' Donna, because your uncle's camping business is going downhill. Fast."

She sat straighter. "That's not true!"

"Oh, but it is." He opened the file, flipped through several pages, and pulled out a sheet. He scanned it, holding it so that she couldn't see what was on it. "In fact, I'd say that if the past season and the current one are any indication, Clearwater Camping is in serious difficulties. Occupancy rates are down, costs are up, and—"

"Occupancy rates? They are not." She faced him indignantly. "I've seen the booking figures for the summer. They're fine. They're right where they should be."

"Bookings may be right where you'd expect them to be. However, a bookings list is one thing. Getting people to stay is another, when the quality of service begins to fail."

While Donna stared at him, her mind whirling, he began reading, quoting figures from a spreadsheet that showed projected revenues. She grew more and more horrified. If what he said was true, by the end of the summer there'd hardly be enough money in the bank to see to the taxes, let alone pay for her aunt and uncle's private nursing home accommodations.

"Let me see that, please," she said, holding out a hand for the paper.

Instead, he slipped the spreadsheet back into the folder and set it on the other side of the sofa. To reach it, she'd have had to fling herself across his lap. Clenching her hands on her own lap, she glared at him.

"Where did you get that information?" It was the first time she'd heard of a drop in occupancy rates! And if she—and Uncle Tyler—didn't know about it, how would he? "My uncle gets a monthly report from the manager of the campground. The last one showed none of that."

But, she thought, the last report had reflected May's receipts, and June's weren't due for another week. What if Gray Kincaid's figures were true and people had been turning around and leaving through the entire month of June, due to poor conditions? If things were as bad as Kincaid made out, it wouldn't become apparent immediately, would it? Still, it was early yet. Even if June turned out to be as poor as May had been—Uncle Tyler had attributed that to the weather—it was in July, August, and September that they made the money that kept the business running.

"Where did your figures come from?" she asked again.

"When we prepare a bid," Gray said, feeling like a rat as he watched worry and confusion play over Donna Mailer's lovely face, "we naturally do a certain amount of investigating. No one stays in business long by buying pigs in pokes." Damn! What was the matter with him? He wasn't supposed to sound apologetic. Or to feel that way.

"That may be true," she said heatedly, jumping up from the sofa and striding away from him. "But I refuse to believe that you have information my uncle lacks. If the campground was in financial trouble, he'd be the first to know it." She whirled back. "He owns it!"

Again, that one eyebrow tilted upward. "Oh? I understood from what he said that you now own it."

She looked distinctly uncomfortable. "In a manner of speaking, maybe."

"*Legally* is the manner in which I was speaking. Are you, or are you not, the legal owner of Clearwater Camping?" His manner suggested that if she wasn't, he was wasting his time talking to her.

Donna glared. Oh yes, his true Kincaid colors were showing now. What had happened to a friendly discussion over a cup of coffee to make the business run smoother? He hadn't even touched the cup he'd poured for himself. Her mouth was now so dry, she had to restrain herself from reaching for it. If only she could get a look at what he had in the folder. It might, she thought, be nothing more than blank pages. Maybe the whole thing was a bluff calculated to scare her into selling for whatever price was offered. That sounded like a Kincaid move.

"Yes, I'm the legal owner," she said. "My uncle sold me the property for one dollar and 'other valuable considerations,' but only because he's afraid he might die at any moment—his heart's not good—and his wife's affairs, since she has Alzheimer's disease, would be taken over by the Public Trustee." She raised her chin another notch. "A Public Trustee who might, in the absence of any other offer, accept your company's blatant attempt at outright theft!"

Her words enraged him, and he shot to his feet. "Neither my company nor I have ever been accused of theft," he all but shouted before he forced himself under control. "And if you'd get down off your high horse and listen, Ms. Mailer, you might find our new offer more to your liking."

Donna paced to the door of his office and back again, halting only a few feet from the sofa. She pinned him with a frigid stare. "I doubt that. Especially when you preface your offer with a bunch of lies about how poorly the business is doing, as if you intend to use that as an excuse to try to get something for nothing."

"I'm not trying to get something for nothing. I'm trying to arrange a business transaction that will satisfy both parties. Of course, I work for my father. He trusts me to negotiate to his advantage. But that doesn't mean I'm out to cheat you or your uncle."

"Doesn't it?" She moved closer, careful not to let her gaze rest on the folder for even a second. Surely, if she managed to grab it, he'd be too much of a gentleman to snatch it back. As big and as muscular as he was, he didn't look like a man who'd use physical violence against a woman. "By your own admission," she went on, "you work for your father, a man who has tried on many occasions to get my uncle's business off Cordoba Island by any means he could devise. You say he trusts you. Fine. That doesn't mean I have to. And my uncle trusts *me* to administer his affairs faithfully, see to the sale of the property, and manage the income from that sale so that he and my aunt can stay in the nursing home for as long as needed."

When she was within one step of the couch, and as if he'd known her intentions all along, Gray put a hand on her shoulder. She felt its heat, its hard texture, as if her silk blouse didn't exist. Despite the warmth of his palm, a shiver danced down her back. "For Pete's sake," he said, "what are we doing, exchanging insults? That won't get either of us anywhere. Let's sit down again and discuss our business rationally. This conversation seems to be getting a bit too heated."

"It's not getting anything of the sort," she said, jerking her shoulder free. Something told her she might never be able to discuss business—or anything else—rationally while Gray Kincaid was touching her. "I'm simply trying to make you see my side of things. Aunt Sadie is sixty-eight and Uncle Tyler is seventy-three. Either one of them could live another ten or twenty years. So I must get the best possible deal for their property in order to provide for their needs in the future."

"And I must get the best possible deal for Kincaid Developments," Gray said, tapping the portfolio impatiently on one thigh. "Since you haven't even heard our second offer, I don't know why you're so intent on justifying an immediate refusal."

"And as I said, you seem to be trying to justify making a lousy offer before you even make it. So go ahead, Kincaid. You know the price we want. Let's see how close you can come to meeting it. Make your offer."

He made it and she laughed, because she felt such a strong need to cry. So much for Uncle Tyler's high hopes that maybe this time Chester Kincaid had decided to play fair.

"Not a chance, Kincaid. That's barely ten percent higher than your April offer."

"Not much has changed in two months, except that Clearwater Camping is having an even more disastrous season than it had last year." He paused to draw in a breath, then said with obvious patience, "Come on, Donna, admit it. You can't rely on the old standard of 'business goodwill' to boost your price. Goodwill exists only if the business is doing well. Yours is not."

"If Clearwater Camping had a bad season last year," she said, more angered by his forbearance, which she found patronizing, than by his statement, "it was merely because the weather was the absolute pits and the fish didn't show up in their normal abundance. That happens in the camping industry, especially in a campground geared to sports fishermen with trailerable boats. That does not mean the business is going under! And you're wrong to say that not much has changed, Graham Kincaid. Plenty has changed!"

She slung her purse over her shoulder, nearly clipping him in the elbow with it. "I've come home, for one thing, and I'm not going to stand around and watch a couple of greedy developers cheat my relatives out of what they deserve. Especially greedy, cheating developers named Kincaid. The Kincaids have already cheated me out of too much as it is!"

His eyes snapped with sudden renewed fury. "What the hell does that mean? I've never cheated anyone. That's not the way I do business."

His anger bounced off hers. "No? You're Chester Kincaid's son, aren't you? Cheating's in your blood! You're trying to get my uncle's property for as little as you can possibly squeak by on, and you're even prepared to lie about the state of the business in order to do it. If that's not cheating, then what the hell do you call it?"

Gray slowly counted to ten. Then fifteen. He shouldn't let this woman get under his skin, but dammit, he hated being called a cheat. Even more, he realized he hated *her* thinking he was a cheat.

"I'm not lying about anything," he said. "The reports I have here are genuine. Donna, please. Trust me on this."

"Trust you? A Kincaid?"

"Trust me. *Gray* Kincaid."

"All right." She challenged him. "So show me. Where did you get them? Who do you have spying on my uncle's business?"

That, he knew, was not something he could discuss with her, anymore than he could let her see the reports. Dammit, his father had set this up. Gray didn't like it one bit, but still . . . The information was undoubtedly true, and he had it, so that was what he had to base his offer on. Dammit, he wished he could show her the figures his father had acquired. It wasn't fair, asking her to do business when she didn't have all the information she needed. It was no wonder she thought he was lying or trying to cheat her.

He frowned, thought hard for several moments, then said, "Listen, why don't you go out to Cordoba Island and look around for yourself and—"

"No!" The single word, a harsh whisper, cut him off. Her face paled, and instinctively he reached for her, steadied her. She twisted free of his clasp and shook her head. "No," she said again, staring at him, eyes filled with something he didn't fully understand, but he thought he saw horror there, or fear, or grief. Whatever, her eyes were huge and wounded and so beautiful, his breath snagged in his throat. He ached with the need to erase the distress she so clearly felt. "I . . . can't!"

"Can't?" He frowned. "Why not?"

Donna bit her lip as she fought to bring herself back under control. What an idiot she was, letting a mere suggestion throw her like that. It wasn't as if Gray Kincaid were in any position to force her to return to Cordoba. All the man had done was suggest that it might be to her advantage, for heaven's sake!

"I won't have time," she said quickly, hoping he wouldn't notice her too rapid, too shallow breathing. "I have to . . . look for a job. And a place to live, of course. I'm staying in a bed-and-breakfast now, so—" She broke off with a helpless shrug, knowing she'd been babbling to try to cover her consternation. It was better to shut up than go on making a fool of herself.

Gray stared at her, concerned. "What's wrong?" he asked softly. He again put his hands on her shoulders, feeling the delicacy of the bones under his palms. He wanted to draw her against him, stroke her hair, give her his strength to rest on, make whatever was wrong, right.

"Nothing!" she said, but he knew it was a lie. She stiffened under his hold, and her eyes got that wild, panicky look again. With difficulty, he refrained from pulling her into his embrace, knowing that she would reject comfort from him. Her shoulders quivered, her chin tilted stubbornly. He saw her mouth twist as she forced a smile that hurt him deep inside with its terrible, aching sadness.

"What I mean is," she said with an attempt at lightness, "there won't be any need for me to go there." She smiled again, stepped free of him, and shrugged. "We'll sell the place, to you or someone else. Why waste time and ferry fare?"

Something basic, primal, made him insist. "Why don't you want to go there?"

She glared at him and said with a hint of desperation in her tone, "It's not that I don't want to go there. I simply want to sell the place and be done with it. But I can't accept your offer. It's too low."

"Donna, believe me," he said sincerely, urging her to sit again on the sofa with him, "it isn't too low. Not the way things are now. I wouldn't make an offer I didn't think was fair."

Dammit, he wished he knew some way to convince her that she was asking for the moon. And he wished, suddenly, that he had some way of getting the moon for her, if that was what she wanted. Those big, hurting eyes, that beautiful, tremulous mouth, got to him. They made him want to protect her, keep her from all kinds of harm, especially the kind he might have to inflict by not increasing his offer.

"And I'm sure if you went out there and looked around," he added, "as I have, you'd come away convinced that things aren't quite as you remember them."

As she shook her head doggedly, he impulsively

grabbed her hands and held them, looking deep into those incredible brown eyes of hers. "Don't forget, Donna, for the past ten years your uncle has been getting older every day and less able to work hard. The place is run-down. I'm not lying, not trying to cheat you. Clearwater Camping—as a business—is not worth what you think it is."

Maybe he was right about that, Donna thought. Maybe Uncle Tyler had let things go a bit in the past years. If he had, it would be only natural. That was a lot of land for one man to look after, and Aunt Sadie's condition had been deteriorating for at least three years. Uncle Ty must have had to spend a lot of time looking after her.

But the manager he'd hired and trained had a wife and four teenage sons, all on the payroll in one way or another. With that kind of help, the campground should be in top-notch condition. If it wasn't . . .

That still didn't mean she had to give it away!

She snatched her hands free. "All right, assuming the campground is a bit shabby, that doesn't make the *land* less valuable. That's a huge chunk of property."

"For our purposes, the land has little value. It's zoned as a campground, and the Islands Trust won't even consider rezoning to allow us to build housing. Nor can we sell the timber off the back, undeveloped half. Your uncle is aware of that. He tried to get a permit to cut the trees back there. He also tried to get one to develop those eight acres as a subdivision. It was no dice for him, Donna, and it would be the same for us. So no. If we buy your campground, that's exactly what we'll be getting, a rundown campground that will take a lot of money and effort to put back into shape."

Donna narrowed her eyes and leaned back,

thinking fast about what he had just said. This was not information Uncle Tyler had thought to pass on to her, though he might not have realized the significance of it. She'd thought the Kincaids, who ran a development company, naturally wanted the land to develop it. This put an entirely different complexion on things.

"Now that's interesting," she said slowly, meeting his gaze. "If the campground is of so little value, then why in the world do you want it? Why does Kincaid Developments keep making offers?" Her reward for the question was a hint of a flush high on his tanned cheeks.

Gray chewed his bottom lip for a second, then shot to his feet and strode back behind his desk. He slammed the folder down and wheeled to glare out the window.

What the hell kind of a businessman was he, he asked himself angrily, letting slip something like that? If she even suspected how badly his father wanted that campground, she could all but demand her price! Was Freud at work here? When he turned, Donna was on her feet, watching him closely.

Oh, hell, there were no two ways about it. She'd asked a valid question, one he'd put to his father more than once. The answers he'd gotten had never satisfied him, and now he had even more questions caroming around in his head.

He sighed silently. He wasn't, as his father never tired of reminding him, paid to ask those kinds of questions. If his father wanted Tyler French's Clearwater Bay property, then it was Gray's task to try to get it, whether he knew the reasons or not.

"The offer is a valid one, Donna," he said. "And

I'm confident you won't get a better one. Why not take it and end your uncle's worries?"

"Maybe I won't get a better offer this month," she said, poking that cute little chin of hers out another half inch. Suddenly he had the most intense desire to kiss her until she went all soft and warm in his arms, till her lashes fluttered closed and made dark arcs on her pearly skin. He hardened, thinking about that, and was glad the solid width of his desk hid the fact from her.

"And maybe not even this year," she continued. "But I'm prepared to wait until I do get one. Tell your father that. Tell him there's no way he's going to get Clearwater Camping for a song."

Turning on her heel, she headed for the door, swung it open, then looked back.

"You tell him for me, that if he wants it, he's going to have to come up with the whole damned opera."

TWO

As the door slammed shut behind Donna, Gray found himself staring at it while a huge grin slowly grew on his face, a grin that developed into a full-bodied laugh. Flopping down into his chair, he sat back and replayed in his mind every nuance of that meeting with Donna Mailer. He felt fantastic. He felt uplifted. He felt euphoric.

He felt as if he were onto something good.

Half an hour later, he managed to bring himself down far enough to pick up the phone and call his father.

"Hello, Dad," he said. "It's still no go on the campground deal."

The stream of curses that whizzed over the wire should have melted the phone, but Gray waited them out. They always came to an end eventually. When, with an angry snort, his father said, "Dammit, keep trying!" he suggested that Chester come up with a better price.

"I don't think we're going to get it for what you want to pay."

"We damned well will, boy, or I'll find myself another acquisitions man!"

Gray shrugged, knowing his father would hear his lack of concern in his voice. "That's up to you, of course." His father fired him at least three times a month. Sometimes he wondered why he simply didn't stay fired one of these times. The fact was, he felt sorry for the old man. It had been his loneliness since Jamie's death that had brought Gray back into the picture, brought him to work there.

Abruptly, Chester changed his tone, and Gray smiled. The only way to deal with a bully was to refuse to be bullied. Too bad his half brother Jamie had never learned that. "All right, all right," Chester said. "Forget it. I know your heart has never been in getting that property." He paused, as if thinking, then said, much too casually, "I guess I'll just take care of it myself."

"Now wait a minute." Something in his father's voice alerted Gray. Some of Chester's business practices didn't sit well with him—such as paying the campground manager's oldest son to filch the business's figures for him. And now that Donna was involved, a large part of him rebelled completely.

"What do you have in mind?" he asked, not bothering to conceal his suspicion. "Don't forget, you're supposed to be retired, and the new management—me—doesn't go for anything sneaky or underhanded."

"Semiretired!" Chester's voice was an angry bark. "I'm still the president of my own company, boy." Chester figured that as long as he had a phone and a fax machine, no one could accuse him of being fully retired. "Somebody's got to be on hand to do the jobs that you're too lily-livered to handle."

That stung. "Fair business dealings do not equate with lily-livered. Give me a decent budget to work with, and I'll get your damned campground property for you. It will simply take more time and maybe some honesty and goodwill on your part."

"Time?" Chester apparently chose to ignore the crack about honesty. Maybe he realized it was pointless to try to convince Gray that he was honest. Or maybe he simply didn't care. "I'm not spending any more time on that deal," he said. "I'll force that old fool to sell. It will be all over by Monday evening. You watch me, boy. I'll find a way to bring him into line. See if I don't."

"Now wait a minute. There are things you don't—" Gray broke off when he realized he was talking into a dead phone. With another of his long-used business practices, Chester had hung up when he'd said all he intended to say. If Gray phoned back, Maggie, the housekeeper, would be instructed to say that he was "unavailable." It didn't matter whether it was his own son or the president of IBM. If Chester Kincaid didn't want to talk, he didn't talk.

Gray sat there for several minutes wondering what his father was up to, then lifted the phone again and dialed. It rang and rang in Donna Mailer's bed-and-breakfast house, and no one answered.

He set his phone down reluctantly. He'd wanted to warn her. But when it came right down to it, what could he warn her about? What would he say? "Watch out, my father's up to something"?

For reasons he didn't understand—yet—she already distrusted his father, and by extension himself, so why would she believe him? It was, he suspected, more than just a basic distrust of all developers, a distrust shared by much of the public. This suspicion of hers was personal, and he meant to find out what it was all about. Since she had lived far away for a full ten years, it had to be something Chester had done to her aunt and uncle, not to her. But whatever it was, it had been bad enough to make her loathe his father.

He'd call her Monday morning and find some way to get her to see him again. He sighed, wishing that other commitments didn't have him tied up all weekend.

If he could, he'd find a way to convince Donna Mailer that the two of them should get together. Be together. He smiled, remembering the way her pert nipples had hardened within the satin and lace cups of her bra, visible through the thin silk of her blouse. Was all her lingerie as delicate as that? He was sure of it. And he was just as sure that any woman who wore fabrics like that revealed, consciously or unconsciously, her sensual nature. It was a nature he ached to explore.

And that hair of hers, so richly colored, silky, soft, scented . . . Heat shot through him at the mere thought of her, thinking about being with her, having a long, intimate dinner, dancing across a moonlit patio, pausing in the shadows to kiss her perfect mouth, palm those rounded breasts with their hard, sensitive nipples and . . .

Oh, yes. She would be a woman well worth seeing again, and he was going to see her, just as soon as he could arrange it. Monday morning, first thing, he'd call.

"He did *what?*" Donna's heart pounded much too fast. Her hand grew wet and slippery as she tightly gripped the phone. "Last night? Just like that?" She felt sick. Her head spun. "Good grief, Uncle Tyler! We have the First of July long week-end coming up. How could a campground man-ager just up and quit, walk out on a Sunday evening, leaving the place unattended in mid-season?"

"Well, he's done it," Uncle Tyler said. "Mike Jersey phoned me because he didn't know what else to do."

Mike Jersey was a guest who'd been coming to Clearwater Camping for over twenty years. He and Tyler were friends. "And it's a good thing he did," Tyler added.

"Yeah," Donna said heavily. And Tyler had phoned *her* because he didn't know what else to do.

"Don't worry about it, Uncle Tyler. I'll go out to the island." Her voice trembled and she quickly firmed it. "I'll take care of things until the place sells or we find another manager."

"I know you don't want to do that," Tyler said, obviously fretting. "Maybe you *can't* do it. You were just a kid when you lived with us, and you didn't have much to do with the running of the place." He paused. "Maybe we should take Kin-caid's offer."

"No!" Everything in her balked at the idea. "After all, how difficult can it be, running a camp-ground? The hospitality business is the same, no matter what end of the scale you're working at. It's not as if I were completely inexperienced."

"That's true," Tyler conceded, though he still sounded worried. Donna calmed him as best she could, but it wasn't easy, considering that she was anything but calm herself.

After she'd hung up, she sat staring at her

hands for a long time, watching the tremor in them finally begin to fade. She swallowed hard and reached for her lukewarm breakfast coffee, wetting her dry mouth and throat. Sure, she thought. How difficult could it be, running a campground? Not difficult at all, except that particular campground was on Cordoba Island, a place that had figured very strongly in her nightmares for the past ten years.

Quickly, before she could think about it too much, she jumped up and began carelessly stuffing clothing into suitcases. The reason she'd never wanted to return was because she hadn't wanted to risk running into Jamie Kincaid again. But there was no chance of that. Jamie was "dead and gone," as Aunt Sadie had put it in a moment of lucidity the week before.

"And no great loss," Uncle Tyler had added. He'd gone on to explain, with a certain relish, Donna had thought, how Jamie had "rammed his sports car up the tailpipe of a parked semi." Yet, however he had gone and whatever he'd done to her in the past, Donna couldn't help feeling sorrow over Jamie's death. He'd been spoiled and indulged, as well as neglected, and the odd combination had produced someone who was half man, half child, not fully responsible for his own actions. She hadn't known that at the time, though.

To her innocent sixteen, his twenty had seemed sophisticated and adult, and she had loved him for a long time even after she knew she should hate him. Yet how could his love have survived the unremitting verbal battering his father had administered, the threats, the intimidation?

She sighed. If she hadn't been a frightened sixteen-year-old, she might have been able to overbalance the weight of Chester's power, the depth of his fury, to convince Jamie that his father's dire prophecy of enforced poverty didn't matter to her, wouldn't matter to their baby, and shouldn't matter to him. If she had been older, wiser, stronger, would she have been able to sway Jamie back to the promises they had made to each other?

She would never know, and it was pointless to ask.

Jamie had been an immature twenty. When faced with his father's outrage and his mother's hysteria over what was being "done to her darling boy," he had crumbled like a potato chip.

He had denied, in the end, that he could be the father of her baby. He had turned his back on her, walked away, and then, as she leaned broken and ill against the wall, with Uncle Tyler beside her telling her to stand straight and leave proudly, Chester Kincaid had also turned his back on her and his unborn grandchild.

The next week, Uncle Tyler had put her on a bus headed east, her destination an unwed mother's home "where she would be cared for" until it was all over and her child safely in the hands of its adoptive parents.

Better, she'd thought, than the abortion Chester had advocated as a solution to "her little problem."

Since then, Donna had been on her own.

So what's new? she asked herself. *It all happened a long, long time ago. Stand up straight, square your shoulders, and get on out there to take care of that campground. You're sure not sixteen now.*

She zipped her last case closed and hauled it to the door. She may not be sixteen, but Lord, how she hated the idea of returning to Cordoba Island

and all the painful memories she'd worked so hard to eradicate.

For a weak moment, as loneliness assailed her, she wondered if she would ever have anyone she might phone "because she didn't know what else to do." To her shock, the image of Gray Kincaid's strong face, his square jaw and steady eyes, flipped up in front of her like a flash card. Appalled, she squeezed her eyes shut.

No! He was a Kincaid. She had to remember that. She had to remind herself whenever she was in danger of forgetting, that if her daughter had lived, Gray Kincaid would have been the child's uncle. He undoubtedly would have been as eager as Chester and Jamie to deny her very existence, to see her destroyed to protect the precious Kincaid line, and not have it sullied by being mixed with that of a campground owner's niece.

The only reason his image had popped into her mind was because he was the last one to have made an offer for the property. It was tempting to do as Uncle Tyler had suggested and let the Kincaids have the place.

But at any price?

If only Gray's offer had been an adequate one, she would phone him right now and tell him yes, tell him to take over. Tell him that the campground and the problems ownership of it entailed were now all his.

She sighed and opened the door.

No. The problems, she was afraid, were all hers.

Gray tried Donna's number early Monday morning. He received a busy signal three times in a fifteen-minute period, then half an hour later, to his disgust, the phone rang unanswered, until it was picked up by her hostess's answering machine. He left three messages during the day, but it wasn't until Tuesday morning that he finally got a reply—from the landlady, who said Donna had checked out early Monday morning.

"Yes," she said in reply to his request for a forwarding address. "Clearwater Camping, on Cordoba Island."

Now what, he wondered, could have driven Donna to go there on Monday, when on Friday she had nearly collapsed at the very idea? Something had changed, but what? His question as to when Ms. Mailer planned to return elicited the reply that she didn't. "The manager of her uncle's place out there quit," the woman said. "Poor girl. She was fit to be tied."

After thanking the woman and hanging up, Gray sat for several minutes deep in thought. Oh, yes, he was sure Donna had been fit to be tied. And he was just as sure that, in some way he couldn't yet figure out, his father's machinations were to blame for this new twist in the campground story.

"Nan," he said, buzzing his executive assistant, "how do you feel about handling the wrap-up of the mall purchase? I have to go out to Cordoba."

Nan showed no hesitation. "Sure thing," she said. Moments later, poking her head around the door of his office, she asked, "Getting a jump on your vacation or something?"

"Or something."

She looked at him quizzically. He offered no more, and she said, "You go and have a good time. But what about Trish? Will your ex-wife give her up nearly a week early?"

Nan was referring to the fact that his daughter, Trish, planned to spend the month of July with him at his father's place, as they had done for the past three years. He thought about that for a moment. As much as he loved his daughter, he didn't want her on Cordoba just yet. "I'll come back for Trish in a few days."

As he stuffed papers into his briefcase, he wondered if those "few days" would be enough for what he had in mind: finding out what the hell his father had been up to, and convincing Donna Mailer that there was at least one Kincaid she could trust.

And maybe, if he was lucky, more than trust.

This was one incredibly mismanaged campground she was looking at! Donna spent her first hour back at Clearwater Bay touring the place, checking out each individual site, taking note of the piles of litter; the cracked, stained, wobbly picnic tables; the unraked gravel and overgrown bushes. She spent the next two hours cleaning bathrooms.

What they really needed was a thorough scrubbing from floor to ceiling, and a paint job. Why hadn't that been done before the season started? Why had the overall upkeep been neglected so badly with six people on the payroll?

Sighing gustily, she threw up her hands and left the last bathroom she'd cleaned. Beyond what she'd already done, there wasn't much more to be accomplished there, at least right now. By tomorrow morning, though, she was going to have to have a crew of people to do some of the work that had been neglected.

She divided the afternoon between calling numbers in the work-wanted section of the classified ads, and going over the books. Frequently, she buried her face in her hands as the facts came to light, facts she wished she didn't have to face. Bills had not been paid, often in months. Dunning notices littered the surface and were stuffed in the pigeonholes of her aunt's once-neat rolltop desk. The current account held barely enough money to meet the payroll of the people she knew she'd need to hire and to pay off outstanding debts. The appalling number of empty sites meant she could expect little cash flow for the foreseeable future. It was not a happy picture.

She was grateful she'd had so little on which to spend her earnings over the past ten years. Her savings were going to be sorely tested, though, if she meant to redeem the campground and keep her aunt and uncle in the home.

As the light faded Donna wandered down to the beach. She sat on a log and watched the water roll in, gold-tinged from the fire of the setting sun. Against that fading streak of fiery sky jutted the point of land where the Kincaid house stood. A figure moved across one of the decks, walked down a level and paused, then descended yet another flight of stairs to the stone seawall that skirted the rocky shore.

Donna swallowed. Was it Gray Kincaid? She had thought, foolishly she now realized, that she might hear from him over the weekend, and had wondered what she'd do if she did. If he'd asked her out, would she have gone? Would the attraction she felt for him, combined with the loneliness she'd suffered since moving west again, have overcome the fact of his being a Kincaid? And was it fair, distrusting a man simply because of who his father was, and what his brother had been and done?

He didn't even know—or had claimed not to

know—that Tyler had a niece, so how could he know that she had once lived on Cordoba Island, had once loved his brother and born his baby? If he knew, would it influence his opinion of her?

No matter what, she knew she wanted his opinion of her to be good. She shivered, remembering the feel of his hands on her shoulders, the intensity of his silver-gray eyes. Eyes that had looked into hers as if he were capable of reading her every thought, her every desire. Lord! Desire . . . Her throat tightened as she recalled his smile when he'd glanced at her erect nipples. It hadn't been triumphant, coarse and bawdy, but pleasure-filled, amazed, and wryly amused all at the same time. It had been the kind of smile a man might give a woman as they acknowledged a mutual delight. The kind of sharing and understanding a lover might give his mate when something unexpectedly good happened between them, something that moved them both.

She sighed. Gray Kincaid as a lover . . . She hadn't had many of those, but something deep inside told her that he could very easily be the ultimate one. . . .

Sighing again, she got to her feet and returned to the house, which, mercifully, the manager and his family had not used and was therefore habitable. Reality was something she had to face, and it included a long, hard haul to get this place operational. She didn't have time for illicit dreams, foolish fantasies, about a man who, even if he were as attracted to her as she was to him, would never admit publicly to wanting her.

If he did, his father would soon turn him around. She'd seen Chester Kincaid in action. If he hadn't liked Jamie getting involved with her, he certainly wouldn't tolerate Gray's doing the same. So the best thing to do was forget the man, forget she'd ever met him. The only thing she really wanted from him was a decent, equitable price for this campground, so she could turn her back on it and walk away, leaving all the memories and all the pain behind.

"Ms. Mailer?"

Donna gladly brought her hand down from over her head and rubbed her aching shoulder, smearing more white paint on herself. It wasn't even halfway through the afternoon on Tuesday, her second day at Clearwater Camping, and she was already so tired she could have cried.

"I'm in the fourth shower stall, Andy," she called to one of the boys she'd hired the day before. Andy, having worked for her uncle the past couple of summers, was good to have around. He, at least, knew what had to be done and was willing to set to and do it with a minimum of supervision.

"There's some guy here wants to see you," Andy said.

"A guest?" She hoped so. Another creditor, she didn't want to know about.

"No."

"All right. I'll come out." She set her paint roller on the tray and began to back down the ladder. She halted when she felt a pair of large hands wrap around her waist. "Andy! I can get down—"

"Hi." Gray turned Donna around, grinning at her sudden state of confusion, her wide eyes and slightly parted lips. If he hadn't held her, she would have backed right into an open can of paint. She wore a pair of cutoff jeans that looked as if they might be a relic of her youth, a gray tank top of the same vintage, with one strap falling off her shoulder, and had a brightly patterned scarf tied Gypsy fashion around her hair.

He knew it was too soon, but he couldn't help himself. He knew it might blow his whole case, but it was something he had to do. He bent forward and kissed her.

Donna froze as Gray lowered his head and placed his lips gently, sweetly, yearningly, over hers. She held her breath as they lingered, teasing, making hers tingle and grow warm before he finally pulled away, leaving her weak and shaken . . . and wanting more. She knew that in some circles, a kiss was a standard, casual greeting. But she didn't move in those circles, and his kiss hadn't felt the least bit casual to her. It had, however, set a standard she thought might not be easily met by anyone else.

"I've been wanting to do that since the moment we met," he said, stepping back, his hands sliding down her arms until he held her hands. "And I plan to do it again, better, at a more appropriate time."

He paused as he studied her, his gaze lingering on her lips. "Make that 'times,'" he added softly.

Donna couldn't think of a single thing to say. Her mind was a blank. Her heart was beating too rapidly and her lungs felt constricted. She only stood there, her hands within his, and looked into his eyes. What was happening to her, and why wasn't she making a much stronger effort to stop it?

He let one hand go and rubbed the tail end of her scarf between finger and thumb, the side of his hand caressing her neck. "Silk," he said, and smiled. "Even wearing denim, you have to have your bit of silk, don't you?" His voice softened to an intimate rumble. "Is there more silk . . . else-where? Or satin?"

She drew in a shuddering breath and pulled her other hand free. Stepping away from him, she dragged herself out of her stupefaction.

"Does—does your father know you're here?" she asked.

He blinked. "My father?"

"Yes. You know. The male parent most people have at one time or another in their existence. In your case, the man who employs you. The man who would be most unhappy to know that you were consorting with the . . . With me."

"My father doesn't give me orders, Donna."

She swallowed hard and climbed three steps of her ladder again, looking down at him as she picked up the paint roller. "You work for him." If it sounded like an accusation, she couldn't help that.

"I'm on vacation."

"What a place to spend it!"

"On Cordoba Island? I spend most of my vacations here."

"In a shower room." She had to laugh. Could it be true that he didn't care what his father thought?

His chuckle was warm and sensual, as warm and sensual as his kiss had been, and it sent shivers along her spine. "If that's where you are, Donna Mailer, that's where I want to be. Got another roller? Looks like you could use some help in here."

She stared in surprise, then her gaze flew to where her painting supplies lay stacked in a wheelbarrow. She could use some help in here. She could use some help all over the campground. But from a Kincaid?

"Go home," she said tautly. "Please. Don't do this."

He swung the door of the shower stall wider. "Don't do what, Donna?"

"Don't—don't make me like you."

His hand slid up her calf to curl behind her knee. "Am I so unlikable?"

She shuddered at the sensation of that hard, callused palm on her skin. His gaze held hers, demanding an answer. "No." It was a tense whisper. "But . . ." She sighed and looked away, then applied her roller to the ceiling again.

"But I'm Chester Kincaid's son?"

She glanced down and nodded. "He wouldn't like knowing you're here. Offering to help me."

"He doesn't even know *you're* here, so there's no danger of his knowing I'm helping you." Gray was still unclear in his own mind why he'd failed to tell his father that Tyler's niece had come to take over the campground. Maybe it was simply because he thought his father, after his despicable action, didn't deserve to know. He deserved, instead to sit over there and stew, waiting in vain for the call he was so certain he'd get when Tyler French caved in.

"I'm here because I choose to be," he said. "Because I want to be. I want to get to know you."

She dipped her roller and stepped up another rung, forcing his hand to fall to her ankle, then free. She missed its warmth and gritted her teeth in anger. "Why? So you can seduce me into lowering my price?"

He shook his head. "I no longer want to buy Clearwater Camping."

That was the truth. He had no further interest in buying the campground, not after his last conversation with his father.

He'd sought Chester out as soon as he arrived at his father's house. "You bought off the campground manager!" he'd said without preamble, making no attempt to hide his contempt. "Paid him to quit so Tyler would have to sell."

"That's right," Chester said without a hint of guilt. "How did you find out?"

"Never mind how I found out! I did, and I don't like it."

Chester shrugged. "It's too late to do anything about it now. And even if it weren't, I wouldn't change it. I told you I'd force the old curmudgeon to sell. But I'm not making him any more offers. Let him come to me. Don't worry. Tyler French will be calling me before the week's out. And his price will be a lot lower than before."

Gray smiled. "Don't bet on it," he said, and swung away from his father. "And by the way, I quit."

Now he gave Donna another level look and backed out of the stall. Collecting a roller and a tray, he began on the back wall of the washroom, whistling softly as he worked.

"Why are you doing this?" she asked twenty minutes later when, finished with that wall, he'd started on the one over the row of basins, still without speaking another word.

He wiped a dribble of paint off a mirror. "I told you. I want to be with you, get to know you." He didn't say, *And I have a deep need to make amends for my father's treachery,* but that was certainly a part of it. But, he thought, watching her stretch to reach a corner with her roller, a very small part of it. Mostly, he simply wanted to be near her.

She didn't answer for a long time. After repositioning her ladder to begin the second half of the ceiling, she said with some annoyance, "How can two people get to know each other if they don't even talk?

"I'll talk," he said easily. "Anytime. Name your subject."

To Donna's utter horror, one word popped out. "You."

Three

As if sensing her discomfort and wanting to spare her, Gray turned away and said, "That's easy." He fumbled through the wheelbarrow and came up with a narrow brush. Working carefully, slowly, he began painting the trim around the mirrors. "Product of a broken home, once married, now divorced, father of one child. Anything else you want to know, just ask."

Donna sat on the top step of the ladder watching him work, rubbing her shoulders. Once married, now divorced, father of a child? she repeated silently. There were a million things she wanted to ask, yet for some perverse reason she asked a question to which she already knew the answer.

"How old were you when your parents split up?"

"Under a year," he said.

"That must have been difficult." For whom, she didn't say.

"Not for me. My mother remarried eighteen months later, so I never remember not having a stepfather."

She looked up at the ceiling, dreading lifting her

arm again. Putting it off for the moment, she asked, "Didn't your father have visitation rights?"

Gray smiled wryly, then he reached up for her and swung her down from the ladder. She stared at him, mesmerized as he bent and brushed a light kiss over her mouth. He handed her his little brush, set her aside, and climbed the ladder himself.

He swept the roller across the rough wood, and splatters dropped little white freckles all over his face and arms. "Yes, my father had visitation rights, but he chose not to exercise them until I was well out of diapers. But I had a great stepfather and a pretty normal upbringing."

She tilted her face up to look at him. "What constitutes a 'normal' upbringing?"

"Watch what you're doing with that brush. You're painting a faucet," he said. As she quickly wiped the brass fitting clean, he went on. "Limited allowance augmented by my paper route; sharing a bedroom with my stepbrother until he went to college when I was fifteen, whereupon a younger stepbrother moved in to share with me; fighting with my stepsister for bathroom time; and babysitting the little kids as needed."

She stared at him. Baby-sitting? She tried to picture Jamie baby-sitting and came up blank.

"Do you like kids?" he asked out of the blue.

She smiled. "Of course!"

His laugh warmed her. "You say that as if you were silently adding, 'Doesn't everyone?'"

"Doesn't everyone?" she asked mischievously, then added, "Was it a happy childhood?" She thought of how unhappy Jamie's had been. Maybe that was what had made the two brothers so very different, Jamie glum and pessimistic, Gray cheerful and outgoing.

He smiled. "Sure it was happy. I probably didn't think so at the time, but I know now that it was."

"Jamie mentioned that you had a huge family."

He set the roller onto the edge of the tray, his brows lifting. "You knew Jamie?"

"Well, yes." Despite what he'd said on Friday about never having heard of her, she was still amazed that this was news to him. His father really had never told him about the dirty little slut next door? Or Jamie? But no, obviously they hadn't.

"I mean, we were next-door neighbors," she said, realizing Gray was looking at her strangely. "It would have been odd if we hadn't run into each other once in a while."

"Next-door neighbors who 'run into each other' now and then don't normally discuss their half brothers' families," he said, resuming painting. "What I meant was, were you and Jamie friends? Did you spend time here as a child or something? Visiting?"

Donna hesitated. He really didn't know a thing about . . . anything. For some reason, she liked it that way. "Yes," she said. "We were friends. We . . . played together." That, she knew, was as good a description as any for their relationship. They'd played at being many things—spies, ship-wrecked sailors, lovers, adults. Whatever they had done together had been nothing but playacting. It had only seemed real to her. "I was sorry to hear of his death," she added.

"Thank you," Gray said automatically, watching her closely. He saw the wariness in her eyes, the aloof tilt of her chin as she flicked a glance at him. So, she and Jamie had played together as children. He was too aware of Chester's innate snobbery. Did she think he was cut from the same cloth? Did that account for her initial distrust of him, for her continued and ill-concealed dislike of his father? Had Chester forbidden a couple of innocent kids their friendship because of his in-grained belief in "position"?

And why the hell had no one—for "no one" read "Dad"—ever mentioned to him that the Frenches had a niece, their only relation, living in the East? He frowned as the thought crossed his mind that, knowing Tyler had a relative who would inherit someday, his father had figured he'd be smart to buy the campground property sooner rather than later.

"Don't look so fierce," Donna said, and he heard hurt in her voice. "I'm well aware of your father's feelings about my friendship with Jamie. I don't expect you to applaud me for it either."

"I'm glad to know you and my brother were friends," he said gently. "I don't think he had many."

She looked startled and met his gaze for an instant before continuing with her work. "He . . . didn't. What friendship we shared, we sneaked. He'd built a platform in a huge maple tree up in the back." She gestured toward the undeveloped part of the property. "Sometimes guests would start scrub ball games in the meadow beyond the orchard, and Jamie would climb into the tree through its hollow trunk, up a ladder he'd built, and watch, pretending he was a spy and they were the enemy. I spotted him one day and followed him into the tree."

She laughed as she glanced at Gray's reflection in a mirror. He was staring at her, his roller still again. "Jamie wasn't very happy to have been found out, but I promised not to tell and he couldn't very well kick me out. The tree was my uncle's. Over the rest of that summer, we built a treehouse on his platform. It was a great hideout."

As she finished the trim around the mirrors and crouched to do the facing of the counter, Gray smiled in appreciation of the sight of her sleek legs in their short, tight cutoffs. He wouldn't mind finding a hideout he could share with her. Of course, Jamie wouldn't have seen her as a woman.

"I didn't know Jamie as well as I should have," he said as he rolled paint into the last corner of the ceiling. He backed down the ladder and set the tray on the counter. "I spent very little time with him and my father."

"Yes. So Jamie said." Finishing the front of the counter, she sidled away from him and quickly began rolling paint on the inside walls of one of the cubicles.

"Did you live here as a girl?" he asked as he started on the next stall. "Or just spend summers with your aunt and uncle?"

"I lived here for a few years," she said in a tone that didn't invite any more questions. "What kinds of things did you do in the summer?"

He kept her entertained with stories of his teen years and his family. By the time he was finished, the entire room gleamed with fresh paint.

Meeting him by the counter, Donna poured paint thinner into the tray she'd been using and squished her roller back and forth, cleaning it. "How many were there in that 'huge' family of yours?" she asked, giving him a sidelong glance. "It seems to me you've mentioned about fifteen siblings."

He laughed. "Nah, but believe me, it sometimes seemed that way. We were seven kids in total, which I considered outrageous even in those days. Leith, my stepfather, has a son three years older than me and a daughter a year younger from his first marriage. My mom contributed me, and then the two of them produced four more over the next eleven years. You should see us now when we're all together, what with all our offspring ranging in age from their teens down to a few months. Fifteen doesn't half cover it."

Did he take his son, or was it a daughter, Donna wondered, to those family gatherings, or did they come there all the time? It hit her then that his child would have been her daughter's cousin, that the two children might have been friends. Another crazy thought nearly tilted the balance of her mind. What would have happened to her relationship with Jamie, if they'd gotten married and then she'd met his older brother? She crushed the question down.

"That—that must make for wonderfully riotous Christmases and Thanksgivings," she said quickly.

"Yeah." He grinned and sloshed his roller into the solvent. "But when I was growing up, it also made for skimpy Christmas stockings and overcrowded quarters, none of which I cared about unless I'd just been to visit Dad and had seen Jamie's bedroom. Bedroom suite, I should say."

He shook his head, chuckling. "I must confess, it was awfully hard for me not to envy him all he had."

Donna rinsed her hands in the paint thinner, scraping at deposits around her nails, then moved to one side to allow Gray to clean his own hands and arms. "Do you know how much he hated that room?" she asked as she wiped her hands on a rag.

Gray looked at her in sharp disbelief. "No. What was to hate?" He took the rag from her and carefully dabbed at splatters of paint on her cheeks and chin.

"He had everything a kid could possibly have wanted," he said as he dabbed, "including an intricate train-set with its own mountains and rivers and lakes—complete with real water, I might add. Plus a library of books many small towns would envy, his own television and phone, every toy he could have asked for, and, when he was in his teens, a computer setup to rival IBM head-quarters!"

He dipped the rag into the solvent again and scrubbed gently at the top of her left ear. "So what was to hate?" he repeated.

Donna found a clean cloth and attacked his splatters. "That he couldn't bring his friends to his home," she said slowly, remembering the anger, the bitterness, that had colored so much of Ja-mie's conversation. "That he wasn't even sup-posed to *have* friends locally." She turned his face with one hand on his chin, tinglingly aware of the prickle of his whiskers on her palm, and trying desperately to ignore it as she continued to re-move paint. "That his parents were seldom there even during his vacations from boarding school, and he was alone except for . . . servants."

Her voice cracked and she spun away from him, turning on the water and letting it run warm before soaping her hands and scrubbing them together.

When she dared risk it, she looked at him in the mirror. His eyes glittered and there was a faint flush on his cheekbones. "He hated that room and the pool and the tennis courts and the rest of it," she said, "because he was supposed to be grateful for everything he had. It was supposed to keep him busy and occupied and prevent his wanting other things."

Gray raised his brows. He turned on the tap in the sink beside hers, washing his hands and then his face, puffing and spluttering and blowing as he rinsed. "What other things were there left to want?" he asked, lifting his dripping face and looking at her. "I know for a fact Dad encouraged him to bring friends home with him from boarding school, but he wouldn't."

She tossed him an unused rag. "He didn't have friends at school, Gray," she explained. "Nobody liked him."

He went very still. That was the first time she had ever used his name, and he liked the sound of it on her lips. He drew in a tight breath as he wet another clean cloth under the tap. He rubbed soap on it, then gently wiped her face to remove all traces of solvent. "Rinse," he ordered. When she had done so, he tossed her the last dry cloth.

"He was lonely," Donna went on. "As lonely as I was, which was why, in spite of the fact that most sixteen-year-old boys would rather drink cyanide than be caught in the company of a skinny twelve-year-old girl, we became friends."

Sixteen? That shocked Gray. He knew his brother had always been young for his age, but he sure couldn't see himself building a treehouse with a neighbor kid at the age of sixteen. Not for the first time, he considered what a lucky escape he'd had, his mother divorcing his father and raising him apart from an overly domineering man. Or was it Jamie's mother who'd been the cause of his inability to grow up? He sighed. Maybe, he thought, it had simply been a basic lack within Jamie. Whatever, when he'd died at the age of twenty-five, he'd still been acting far more like a child than a grown man.

"If he was so lonely," he asked, annoyed to hear a tinge of long-ago resentment in his tone, "why did he go out of his way to make me feel unwelcome when I came to visit?"

Donna looked sympathetic. "I can't answer that, Gray."

"There were less than four years between us," he said musingly. "We should have been friends, but he always acted as if he resented me, distrusted me."

"And wasn't that feeling mutual?"

Gray shrugged. "Sure I resented him. Some. I'm human. I thought the division of wealth wasn't fair, especially when I was a kid—a greedy adolescent. And I have to confess I didn't have a lot of patience for someone I saw as a sulky, spoiled brat who never responded to my attempts at communication."

His mile was crooked. "But you know, in spite of that, I always felt sort of bad that we weren't better friends, just the way I always felt cheated that Dad and I weren't closer. That's why I'm trying harder now with him."

Her gaze narrowed. "I hope he appreciates it."

Gray looked at her quizzically. "You don't like my father, do you?"

"I neither like nor dislike him. How could I? I haven't seen him for years, and prior to that, I probably saw him, except at a distance, maybe twice."

The first time, she thought, had been when she'd gone running to Jamie as he got off the ferry on his way home from boarding school. His parents had whisked him away so quickly, she'd known they'd never approve of his friendship with her. They had left her feeling hurt and humiliated and slightly dirty.

Her stomach lurched as she fought down the memory of her second and last meeting with Chester Kincaid. She hadn't begun to know hurt, humiliation, and abasement until that evening.

Gray slipped his hands around her waist and pulled her against him. "What happened, Donna?" he asked, frowning. "What did my father do to you?"

She flung her head back. "Nothing!"

"Oh, yes, he did something, and I mean to find out what it was."

She bit her lip, then forced a smile. "No. Leave it, Gray. The past is . . . past."

He looked at her hard for a long moment before he said, "There's something you're going to have to understand right now, Donna. It's the future that concerns me. Your future. And mine. Get used to it."

"There is no future, Gray. Not for you and me, not if you meant that as I think you did."

"Maybe there will be, maybe there won't be. But I mean to take the time to give it a chance to develop if it has the slightest chance of doing so. All I'm saying right now is that my father's opinions have no bearing on my feelings."

Donna could have told him that she'd heard that before. Instead she turned and quickly walked away.

He caught her before she'd gone ten feet. "All right, now where?" he asked, trundling the wheelbarrow she'd forgotten in her haste to escape. He had even, she saw as she glanced back, taken the time to replace the sawhorse with the Out of Service sign on it across the doorway.

Because she wanted to cry, she asked crossly, "What do you mean, now where?"

"I mean, what's next on the agenda? Workwise."

She faced him, hands on hips, head flung back. "Workwise," she said, "I have brush to cut, paths to rake, picnic tables to repair, and about nine acres of grass and weeds to mow. But you, I understand, are on vacation. You've done your neighborly bit, Mr. Kincaid. You've also done your filial duty, trying to convince me what a nice guy you are so I'll relent and let you have this poor excuse for a campground at some ridiculous price.

"That," she went on, getting nicely warmed up, "is not going to happen. This place is no longer on the market. Not for any price."

He dropped the shafts of the wheelbarrow and faced her down. "And I told you I no longer wanted to buy it."

"I don't believe you!" she shouted, oblivious of the few guests who might hear. "You're the one with the agenda, Gray Kincaid, not me, and it has nothing, really, to do with helping me. You're spying! I thought on Friday that you were lying about how bad this place was, but I've since learned that your information, wherever you got it, was accurate. Well, to save you the time and the effort of looking further, let me tell you that your report scarcely went far enough. This place is in deep, serious trouble! The bills haven't been paid, so suppliers are more than just reluctant to come. They're refusing outright! That means I have to go to town and buy things like toilet paper and cleaning supplies locally—at retail rates. We don't get garbage pickup anymore, so I have to run out to the landfill site every day or the place begins to smell like a garbage dump. We have no more—"

"Donna—" He tried to break in, but she swept his attempt aside.

"You were right. We have no more goodwill in the community or elsewhere. Some of our clients have been with us for thirty years or more. Their children and grandchildren come to us now— have been coming, I should say—practically for their whole lives. But not recently. We once enjoyed a high reputation for providing pristine conditions at affordable rates. Now we have people coming in, taking a look around, and leaving, spending one night instead of the fourteen they reserved. And because we had those bookings sewed up, or so we thought, we didn't take enough reservations from other guests."

She drew in a furious, tremulous breath. "That hurts, Gray. It hurts the business. It hurts me personally. This is not the Clearwater Camping I remember. What I want to do now is turn this place around. Leaving it in this condition would be the same as vacating an apartment without washing the floors and cleaning the refrigerator. So forget about buying me out. Somehow, I'm going to fix what's gone wrong, and while I'm doing that, I won't have time for you and your stupid, juvenile seduction games."

He frowned at her. "When's the last time you ate?"

She gaped. "When's the last time I *ate*? What the hell does that have to do with anything?"

"You sound as cranky and crabby and tired as my daughter does when she's overdue for dinner." Without a further word, he abandoned the wheelbarrow, picked her up, and marched toward the house.

"Put me down! You have no right to do this!"

"Be quiet," he said.

"I don't have to be quiet! I don't have to mmmph—"

When he finally ended the thorough kiss, she was quiet, apart from the soft little hiccups in her chest. He set her on her feet on the front porch, then wiped her eyes and wet cheeks with the palms of his hands.

"Shall we eat here?" he asked pleasantly. "Or would you like to run into town?"

"I want you to go home!" she cried out. "I want you to leave me alone!"

"Not a chance, sweetheart. Not one single, solitary little chance of that. Now, where do you want to eat?"

"I don't want to eat!"

"Okay, then, we'll go inside and make love." He grinned. "For the first time in my life, I find the smell of paint thinner a very definite turn-on."

Donna stared at him. "You're something else, you know. You are something else altogether, Gray Kincaid."

He nodded. "And don't you forget it."

"What part of the Maritimes did you live in?"

Donna glanced up from her menu. "Sydney, Nova Scotia."

"That was a long way from home."

She smiled. "It became home. I lived there longer than I lived here."

"What did you do there?"

"I was an innkeeper."

"No!" He chuckled. "You couldn't be. Innkeepers have thick arms." His fingers wrapped around her slender wrist and slid up toward her elbow, showing her the room to spare. "They have bald heads." He touched her hair with his free hand, combing his fingers under it, lifting it and letting it fall to her shoulder. In her white slacks and bright blue shirt, she looked clean and crisp and delectable among the rumpled fishermen, yachters, and tourists who shared the small, very casual restaurant with them. "They also have potbellies under stained canvas aprons. They fix leaky plumbing and wipe up suds and rent out dingy upstairs rooms to people with shadowy faces and nefarious purposes."

Her laughter rang out, then she nodded solemnly. "That's what I looked like when I was keeping my inn."

As he laughed, too, Donna slipped her wrist out of his warm clasp before she could succumb to the temptation to turn her hand over and link her fingers with his. What was there about this man that made her want to hold hands with him like an adolescent? His fingers slid through her hair again, and as she tossed her head restlessly, his hand fell away. She thought she could still feel its warmth close to her shoulder, though. Or was that simply a result of her overcharged senses? Would she ever be the same, after being picked up and carried home and kissed totally senseless on the way?

And how, after that, had she ended up having dinner with a man she had sworn to resist? There were simply no answers.

"I've never seen anyone less like my idea of an innkeeper than you," he said. His smile sent a wave of butterflies dancing inside her—and a warning siren warbling in her mind. Somehow, the sound of butterfly wings became louder than the warning.

"Still, that's what I do—did."

Gray watched the wistful smile play over her

mouth and wanted to kiss her again. Maybe it was a good thing she hadn't had anything but one dark brown banana and a box of cereal in her house, forcing them to dine out. Otherwise, he might have made good his threat to take her inside and make love to her. "Did you enjoy inn-keeping?" he asked.

"Mmm-hmm. I worked in a beautiful little place called Seaspray Inn. Weathered clapboards, lots of gingerbread, lace curtains, and faded rugs with cabbage roses all over them. Really, it's not much more than a glorified bed-and-breakfast, though we do provide all meals for our guests. There are only nine rooms, each one filled with antiques. There's a tower at one corner, a widow's walk on the roof, and a huge latticed verandah overlooking the harbor."

"You love it."

She nodded. "On foggy nights I'd lie in bed and listen to the nearest foghorn sing. In that way, it reminded me of Cordoba Island. Like the Gulf Islands, it's a place people go to find quiet, solitude. And peace. But there's something more, something about Seaspray Inn that's very . . . healing." She paused, gazing into a far distance Gray couldn't see. "Something almost magical."

The server brought the wine he'd ordered, and Gray sipped at it. Listening to her, he knew that she had been seeking all of that when she'd gone, and had found it there. "Were you at the inn a long time?"

She nodded again. "Yes. Nearly nine years."

That startled him. Almost the full time she'd been away? And a girl as young as she'd been then had needed solitude, peace, a place of healing? Why?

"Was that where you went when you . . . left your aunt and uncle's home?"

Unconsciously, she sighed. "Not right away, but . . . soon after I left, yes."

Six months later, to be exact, she thought, remembering the day she'd been released, weak, exhausted, bereaved, and bewildered, from the unwed mothers' home. They had given her the small sum of money left over from what her uncle had sent for her care, and suggested she start to look for work immediately. "You need a busy, active life, my dear, so you can begin to forget, learn to look to the future."

The one thing not suggested was that she go home. She'd already known from Uncle Tyler's terse letter in response to hers saying her baby had been stillborn, that she would not be welcome, even without a baby to disgrace him.

At the bus station, she'd bought a ticket for a place as far from home as she could afford to go. Eventually, a bus driver had let her off in front of the Seaspray Inn just outside Sydney, Nova Scotia, telling her it was inexpensive this early in May, and that Mrs. Hammond, the owner, often needed summer help.

Something about Cecilia Hammond's manner, her soft voice and innate sympathy, had thawed Donna's frozen emotions. Under Cecilia's gentle urging, her whole story came out, and she had submitted to the healing tears she had long denied herself. "And now," she'd finished, "I don't even have a home to go to!"

"Of course you do, my darling. You've come home today." Cecilia had packed her off to a small room at the top of the tower, put her to bed with a cup of tea, talked to her, cared for her, showed her that she had, indeed, come home. Three days later, she'd brought Donna a big basket of towels to fold, and from there, things had just happened.

"Donna?" Gray's voice brought her back to the present. "Your salad." She leaned back so the waitress could place her meal before her, and watched Gray dig into his chicken strips.

"So, go on," he said. "Tell me more about your inn."

She brightened, her memories happier now, and stabbed a bright pink shrimp with her fork. "I started in the laundry room and the kitchen, folding linens, peeling vegetables, making salads, and learning."

She shook her head. "I had no idea how much there was to learn. I didn't make much, but I had a roof over my head and someone to . . . talk to. To be with."

"You knew no one in Sydney before you went there?"

"Not a soul." For a second, sadness flickered across her face, prompting him to take her hand in his again. This time she let him wrap their fingers together.

"I'm sorry," he said. "If it was a painful part of your life, don't talk about it."

"But it wasn't," she said, giving his hand a friendly squeeze before she released hers from its grip. "Not once I got to Seaspray Inn. The owner of the inn is a dear old lady who treated me as if I were her own child. I was very happy there." It was true. She hadn't been happy right away, but it had come, and the grief had faded. It was only returning here, meeting a Kincaid, that had brought it all back to the surface.

They ate in silence for several minutes, watching small sail and power boats maneuvering in the bay below, and a ponderous ferry make its way out between the islands.

"What did you do after you learned how to peel vegetables?" Gray asked presently, stirring sugar into his coffee.

"Eventually I was promoted to chambermaid, then waitress and bartender. Later I learned to keep the books, make reservations, order supplies, and in general do everything that needs to be done to keep a small hotel running.

"When Cecilia, the owner, wanted to retire two years ago, she made me manager."

"She'll miss you."

Donna nodded. "And I, her." Her smile faltered, then steadied. "But when Uncle Tyler's letters showed me that he and Aunt Sadie needed me, I couldn't refuse. Cecilia understood that and offered to let me take as much leave of absence as I needed, but I didn't think it would be fair to her. I quit outright and she promoted my assistant.

"He's her grandson and will likely inherit the place someday, and though he's only twenty-two, he's ready for the job. And I was . . . ready to leave. But I like knowing that if I ever want to go back, she'll make a place for me, even if it's only in the laundry room."

She sighed and added softly, "But I will miss them, of course."

Gray saw the grief, the haunted look in her eyes. Perhaps, he thought, whatever wounds she had suffered on the way to Sydney, Nova Scotia, had not been completely healed by the magic of Seaspray Inn.

"The training you got there must be a help to you here," he said.

"It is." She looked down a minute. "And you

were a big help to me today, too, Gray. I'm sorry I was so churlish about it."

He grinned. "No problem. Like I said, I recognize the signs of imminent starvation in the female of the species."

"Does your wife have custody of your daughter?"

"Ex-wife," he corrected her firmly. "Yes. Trish lives with her mother. I get her every other weekend during the school year and every Tuesday and Thursday for dinner."

"I'm sorry. You must miss her."

He smiled. "I do. Trish, that is. I'm all over my ex, though when she left me, it came as a complete surprise. I'd thought everything was fine between us." He shook his head ruefully. "Typical male tunnel vision. 'Fine' wasn't good enough, of course. It never is, and I should have seen it. It was my fault because I was too busy to notice that we'd fallen, not just into a rut, but into two separate ruts, and you know what they say about parallel lines."

Donna nodded, strangely loath to discuss his marriage. "How old is Trish?" she asked.

His face became animated, white teeth flashing, dimple darting in and out. She could see love for his daughter radiating from him. Envy cut into her like a knife, then twisted sharply when he said, "She's nine."

Her own daughter, had she lived, would be nine. Cousins who were the same age might have been good friends. So much had been taken from her! Such a huge loss.

"Trish loves my dad's place," he went on, "so we spend our vacation with him every year. It's a good time for all of us to try to become a family."

"To try?"

"We've never been close, my dad and I, but I'd like to improve on that. It's what he wants, too, and after all, he is my father. He's been lonely since Jamie was killed and Colleen, his wife, left him." He made a face. "He hasn't had much luck with wives."

Donna set her plate aside and sipped her coffee.

"I think you should know, I quit my job today," he said. "Before I came to your place."

Startled, she glanced at him. "Why?"

"Because my father—though I'll never be able to prove it—is behind all your troubles at the campground. The information I had that day in my office, he obtained by paying one of the manager's sons to steal it for him."

She looked at him for a long, quiet moment. "And he paid the manager to quit."

Gray sighed. "That didn't sound like a question."

She smiled faintly. "It wasn't one. I suspected it from the very beginning. Only . . . I thought you were part of it."

"And now?"

"I know you weren't."

"I'm sorry, you know. And ashamed of him."

She reached across the table, linking her fingers with his. "I know, Gray."

He continued to hold her hand as they stood and walked to the exit. He refused to let it go even when he paid the bill. The hostess had to hold the credit card slip still while he signed. At last he led Donna out onto the quiet covered verandah that surrounded the restaurant.

Drawing her into his arms, he gazed down into her face. His was only a hint of pale color in the darkness.

"Gray," she whispered. "Gray . . ."

"You," he said, "are one very classy lady."

She drew an unsteady breath. "I'm a very tired lady." Don't do this, she told him silently. She didn't have the emotional strength to fight back, yet she did nothing to stop him.

He lowered his head until his breath fanned over her face. "Too tired for this?" he asked softly.

She sighed and smiled against his lips. "No. No, I don't think I am."

Four

When Gray finally lifted his head, Donna couldn't move. Never had a kiss been so invasive, stealing inside her and robbing her of all conscious thought, all common sense, and leaving in their place a pounding, primitive urge to take this man home with her.

"Donna . . ." he murmured. She was glad that he sounded as stunned as she felt. "I—I guess I should get you home, huh?"

She nodded, completely unable to speak. As they walked to his car, he continued to hold her hand tightly.

She was calmer by the time he stopped in front of her house. Quickly she opened the door, and just as quickly he opened his. "Good night, Gray," she said. "And thank you. For the dinner. And for your help today."

He came around the car and took her hand again. "I'll see you to your door."

"My door is right there," she said. It wasn't more than five feet away.

"Nevertheless, there might be a big, bad wolf

lurking in the hydrangeas. At least let me hold your hand."

She had to laugh around a yawn as they walked slowly, very slowly, past the hydrangeas. "When I was twelve, Aunt Sadie told me—blushing furiously, I might add—that 'holding hands can lead to . . . other things.' Never before nor since have I heard such deadly import attached to the phrase 'other things.'"

He chuckled as they came to a halt on the porch. "Other things? Now, that really interests me." He smiled, his dimple indenting his cheek. Suddenly she was fighting the most bizarre and intense urge to lean forward and place her lips against it, then to move on to his mouth and feel it moving on hers again, to taste him, to open to him, take him inside.

As if he could read her mind—or her face—he said, "Let's explore some of those 'other things' your aunt warned you about."

Sliding his arm around her waist, he led her to the ancient, split-seamed porch swing she had thought of taking to the dump the day before. Now she knew she should have done it.

"I don't think this is such a good idea," she said with utterly no conviction. They were snuggled together, facing the bay and the many bobbing boats tied to the campground wharves. She could see a dazzle of light zigzagging across the water, reflected from a window in his father's house, a strong reminder of exactly why it wasn't such a good idea for them to do this.

He shrugged and lifted one knee, draping his arm over it. "Then can we just sit here for a few minutes before you go in? Look at that beautiful silver glow on the bay. Isn't that something?" She felt his breath on her cheek as he spoke, and looked at him. The glow on the water, she thought, had nothing on the silver of his eyes.

In the light shining faintly from within the house, his hard legs gleamed below the hem of his shorts. She linked her hands together tightly, because they yearned to curve over his thigh, to test the hardness, soak up the warmth. Oh, help! Had it been so long since she'd touched a man intimately, she had to restrain herself from attacking this one?

Her stomach clenched and her throat tightened. Her heart nearly quit beating as he rocked the swing lightly and took her hand in his again, holding it on his warm thigh, prickly with curly hair. Her head spun slowly as if she'd had too much wine. She had drunk only one glass, though, then nothing but water and coffee. Something else had gone to her head.

"You said you lived here for a few years. Why was that?" he asked, half turning to face her. His knee brushed her thigh. As if he were unaware of how galvanic she found the contact, he leaned back and stretched one arm behind her along the back of the swing. His finger played idly with her hair. "I find it incredible that we've never met before this."

"My parents were killed in a traffic accident near our home in Manitoba when I was twelve. Aunt Sadie and Uncle Tyler took me in."

His hand cupped her shoulder tightly. "Ah . . . hell! I'm sorry, Donna. I shouldn't have asked. What a lousy thing to happen to a kid at her most vulnerable age."

She had to smile. "I think any age is lousy for that to happen. But I survived. My aunt and uncle had a harder time, I think. They were stuck with an adolescent girl without any time to lead up to it, and they were already well into middle age. They had no idea how to deal with me."

"Did you have . . . discipline problems?" Could that have been why she'd left at such a tender age? he wondered. Was she a teenage runaway?

She shook her head. "Not really." Uncle Tyler and Aunt Sadie—and certainly Chester Kincaid— would have considered an unexpected, illegitimate pregnancy a "discipline" problem. She hadn't been disobeying anyone, nor had she meant to be "bad." She and Jamie had simply had a plan. One that had gone terribly awry.

"But there were girl-type practices they simply didn't understand," she went on. "Such as sleep-overs."

He groaned. "I wish I didn't understand about sleep-overs. They are a diabolical invention of mothers, I'm sure, designed to drive fathers right over the edge."

Donna laughed. "That bad, is it? Uncle Tyler wasn't driven over the edge. He just couldn't figure out why I wanted my best friend to spend the night. He looked completely puzzled and said, 'Your friend wants to sleep here? Why? Doesn't she have a bed at home?' Of course, they let me do it, but everyone was so uncomfortable, I never asked again."

He flattened her palm on his thigh, picking up her fingers one by one and letting them fall. "Go on. Tell me more. Who was your best friend?" He lifted a tress of her hair and let it slip slowly through his fingers. It caressed her bare shoulders as it fell. He did it again. And again, as if he knew . . .

She shuddered. "Gray . . ."

"You had a best friend named Gray? How strange."

"Gray," she said again.

He turned his head and smiled at her. His eyes half-shut, he ran the tip of one finger around her ear. "Hmm?"

"Don't . . . do that."

"Don't ask you about your childhood? But you asked about mine earlier today."

"Don't touch me."

He removed his hand unhurriedly, his thumbnail "accidentally" trailing across her upper arm. "Sorry," he said. "Don't you like to be touched?"

"I . . . Yes, but . . ."

"But what?" There was a gentleness in his voice, in his eyes, that made her feel all floaty and unreal, made her ache for that touch she had told him she didn't want.

"But I don't know you," she managed to say.

"And isn't that why we're together? To get better acquainted? What better way to get to know each other than my . . . touching you?" He stroked a hand from her shoulder to her waist. "And your touching me? While we talk."

He took her hand and placed it on his chest halfway up, partly on his shirt, partly on his bare skin. Her fingers, as if with a will of their own, slid off his shirt and curled into his chest hair. Then they splayed out, her palm pressing over the hard beating of his heart.

"When I kissed you after dinner," he murmured, his gaze locked with hers, "your lips answered mine."

She knew that. All too well, she knew that.

"I can't stop thinking about the way you tasted," he said. "The way you felt. Have you been thinking about that kiss, too, while we've sat here?"

Her lips tingled as she thought about it. She licked them quickly. "Yes, but . . ."

Laughter silvered his eyes. "Yes, but you don't like being kissed?" He stroked the pad of one thumb over her lower lip.

"I . . ." The shudder that quivered through her body put a quaver in her voice. This was crazy! She laughed self-consciously. "Damn you, yes! Of course I like being kissed. But—" She broke off abruptly, snatching her hand from his chest. To her dismay, it fell to his thigh. The muscle there was as hard as she'd imagined it would be. Her fingers couldn't resist testing the firmness of that muscle, making him draw in a sharp breath and flatten her hand on his leg again, pinning it there, holding it still, as he stared into her eyes.

"But you don't like wanting to kiss back?" he asked.

She would have leaped to her feet if she thought her knees wouldn't have collapsed. "I don't like wanting to kiss you back."

His smile faded, replaced by a frown. "Why?"

She tossed her head and spoke the first thought that crossed her mind, the first one that made any sense at all, even though she didn't put a lot of credence in it anymore. "Because I have a feeling you're still trying to find a way to make me lower my price on this campground."

He laughed, throwing back his head and spreading his arms wide. "Sounds good, Ms. Mailer, but we both know it's not true. I told you already. I don't want your campground, and even if my father does, he's not going to get it through me. Remember, I quit."

The arm that was behind her swept down and encircled her waist, tilting her toward him across his bent leg. He moved so quickly, she couldn't catch her balance in the swaying swing. He grinned as she fell against him harder than even he had intended, then curled her more comfortably in his arms, his bent leg straightening to make room for her close to his hip.

He caught her hand once more, holding it flat on his palm, watching it tremble. "You're scared." He sounded incredulous. "Of me?"

"Of course not. I simply don't think it's a good idea for us to—"

"To get to know each other?"

"Gray . . ." There was a threat in her tone.

"Say it more softly," he said, bending forward so his lips brushed hers. "The way you did at the restaurant."

"Gra-ay!" For a warning, it sounded far too much like a plea. His lips caressed hers again. This time, hers opened to taste him. Just a tiny taste, she promised herself. Not enough to become an addiction.

"Why are you doing this?" she asked.

"Because I have to. Because I didn't do it properly before, and I've been wanting to since the first moment I saw you."

"Oh."

"Reason enough?" His voice was a low rumble close to her ear.

"I . . . guess." She knew that he was talking to give her time to back off, to tell him no, to think about it if she needed to.

She did need to think.

Trouble was, she didn't want to. She licked her lips. In anticipation? Her stomach clenched again, so hard that it hurt. She shivered. It hurt in the most incredibly wonderful way. It couldn't be called painful, and it needed something very specific to soothe it. Some*one*!

"What was wrong with the way you did it before?" she asked, sounding weak and breathless to herself. "It seemed fine to me."

He smiled. "I believe I've mentioned a lesson I learned the hard way. 'Fine' isn't good enough." One hand slid slowly up her arm, across her shoulder, and cupped her nape. She tilted her head to his as he brushed his lips over hers for the third time. Her heart hammered so hard, she thought it might break her ribs.

"This time it's going to be much, much better than 'fine,'" he murmured.

Donna wondered for a crazy moment why it sounded as if he were talking about something more than just a kiss. But then his mouth took hers, his tongue stroking sensually across her lower lip, dampening it, making it tremble as she trembled inside. She moaned softly in acquiescence, thought processes coming to a full stop.

"Come to me," he whispered, and stood. He exerted a tiny amount of persuasion, just enough to bring her to her feet, to bring her breasts against his chest, her hips in line with his, her thighs nestling close. His hand stroked her throat, fingers lingering on the soft skin below her ear. His eyes, looking silver-blue between his half-closed lashes, smiled . . . and then he kissed her for real.

His lips were hard, purposeful, determined, and she took what they offered, parting her own to allow him access as she slid her arms around him, angling her head to meet him on his terms. It was a deep kiss, a powerful kiss, and it made her head spin, made her insides melt, made her legs tremble. She didn't think she could stand, but his arms swept around her, pinning her to his body so that he held most of her weight, cradling her between his thighs. She felt his hard arousal, reveled in it, ached for it, ached to ease it because that would ease the deep pain inside her.

It was happening much too fast, growing much too strong, spiraling her up toward a point of no return, and she didn't know how to leash it. He sank back onto the swing, drawing her down on top of him. Keeping her wrapped in his embrace, he kissed her again and again, leaving her lips long enough to glide his over her cheeks, her eyelids, her brows, and down the side of the neck before returning to her mouth again.

She clung to his shoulders, and when he released her finally and whispered her name, she murmured his, smiling into his eyes.

"Yes," he said. "That's how I wanted to hear you say my name."

She said it again as she smoothed one of his eyebrows with a finger. "You are right," she added. "That was more than just 'fine.'"

"What was it?" he asked, nuzzling the soft skin under her left ear. "How would you describe it?"

Her breath shivered out of her. "I . . . don't know."

He tilted her head up. "Maybe we need to do it again, so you can find the words?"

"Mmm, yes. Maybe," she agreed.

He simply smiled into her eyes, waiting, and she happily initiated the kiss. When they broke apart, levering themselves into sitting positions, she gazed at him, more deeply shaken and touched than she had ever been before.

"I knew there was a reason I should avoid you," she said.

"And I knew there was a reason I should kiss you like that, show you what you do to me."

"You do something to me too," she said.

Gray didn't want to talk, though. He only wanted to kiss her again under her ear. He seemed obsessed by that spot. When she turned her head, he pinned her to him with both hands on her back.

"You . . . taste . . . wonderful," he said, nipping at her lips. "I knew you'd taste like . . . that, all honey . . ." He tasted again. "And cinnamon and . . ." He had to search, deeply, for the next flavor. "And mint."

Donna opened her eyes slowly, amazed to find that her arms had wound around his neck again. "And wine," she said. "We mustn't forget the wine."

He smiled and looped his long fingers over her elbows, holding her arms around his neck when she would have sought freedom. "Are you blaming the wine you drank with dinner for this?"

She could see he wasn't going to let her get away with that. "No." She slipped away from him and stood, this time making it stick by planting a palm in the center of his chest when he would have overruled her. "No, I'm blaming myself." She laughed. "And you, of course. I do believe you were rather closely involved too."

He grinned. "I do believe you're right."

"And I also believe that it's time for me to go in. This has been a very . . . full day." Besides, she thought, somebody had to cool this wildfire attraction!

"I know. I'll be back tomorrow to work with you."

"Gray! No."

"Donna!" He mocked her. "Yes." That, though, was very serious.

"You don't have to."

"I do have to."

Because he wanted to? she wondered. Or because he felt he had to atone for his father's sins?

"Where are you staying?"

He looked surprised at the question. "At my father's house, of course."

"But . . . I thought you'd quit your job with him."

He laughed and stroked a hand under her chin, down her throat to her collarbone. Her nipples hardened instantly. "I did, but I didn't quit being his son. Trish expects to spend her vacation there. Dad expects both of us to spend the month of July with him." He grinned. "Besides, he doesn't believe I mean it when I say I've quit."

She searched his eyes as best she could in the dim light. "Do you?"

He wanted to be as honest with her as he could possibly be. "I think so, Donna. But a lot depends on his actions over the next few weeks."

"Don't," she said warningly. "Don't use me as any kind of weapon in whatever war you might be waging with your father. I hope I've made myself completely clear."

He nodded. "Completely." After a moment's hesitation, he stepped right up to her, his chest touching her breasts. "Donna, I want another thing made completely clear between us. Whatever the outcome of your friendship with my brother might have been, I am Gray, not Jamie, and I don't want you ever to forget it."

She swallowed hard and moved back away from him. "I don't suppose I will, Gray."

He smiled. "And just to make sure you don't . . ."

Right, she thought, letting him draw her into his arms for another kiss. Somebody had to cool this wildfire attraction.

Clearly, it wasn't going to be her.

• • •

"Where does that trail lead?" Gray shut off the gasoline-powered brush beater and gestured toward a much narrower trail than the one he'd been clearing.

"To the lake," Donna said. "I came to tell you lunch is ready, if you'd like to join Andy and me."

"Great," he said, slapping a mosquito. "I'm starved." He grinned at her. "Would you believe I'm having more fun than I've had in a long time?" He slung the weed cutter over his shoulder and walked along beside her, looking for all the world like an old-time logger with a bucking saw. Donna had to laugh.

"What's funny?"

"You. What's fun about whacking down weeds and getting chewed by mosquitoes?"

He glanced at her quizzically. "You know, I really can't say. But I'm enjoying it. Want me to clear out the trail to the lake next?"

"If you like. Thought not many of the guests fish there anymore. We don't allow power boats in it. It really isn't big enough. Some of our guests bring canoes, though, so they can fish. Or they did. I'm not sure there're any fish in there. I haven't had time to go fishing since I came."

Gray came to a halt, staring at her. "You like fishing?"

"Yes. Why?"

"Because I like fishing too." He took her hand as they walked on. "Would you let me fish in your lake, lady?"

Donna swallowed hard. For some reason, the question had sounded intensely suggestive—or was that simply because Gray Kincaid had asked it, and that he was holding her hand and looking at her in a certain manner that made her heart hammer and her nipples, dammit, stand straight out?

"Sure," she said, as if she hadn't heard a hint of innuendo. "Help yourself. We used to keep a canoe there for our own use, but it's probably rotten now. Still, you can cast from the shore. If you don't have any fly-casting equipment with you, I can lend you some."

"You have fly-casting stuff?"

"Yes," she said as he put the weed cutter in the shed. "One winter, Uncle Tyler even tried to teach me to tie my own flies. I'm afraid I was hopeless, but he forgave me because I was the best fisherman in the family."

They entered her house through the back door. Gray stopped her by tugging on her hand. "You bragging?"

She blinked up at him. After the bright sunlight, the hallway was dim in comparison. Still, she had no trouble seeing that his gray eyes were dancing. "Yeah," she said. "Maybe I am. Why? You challenging?"

He grinned down at her, his dimple flashing. "Sure. Why not right after dinner?"

"Tonight?" She led the way into the kitchen.

"Tonight."

She glanced at Andy, her assistant, who was leaning over a fat book as he munched a thick sandwich. His big, bare feet were crossed under his chair and his elbows were propped on the table. His presence brought her back to reality, reminding her that because of Gray's father's machinations, Andy was the only full-time help she could afford. Not that Gray wasn't helping full-time, and not for wages.

She still wasn't certain she could afford his price, either.

"I . . . uh, no, Gray. I went out last night and I shouldn't have. I can't keep doing that, you know. It's not a good idea to leave the place unattended. What if somebody needs something?"

He looked at her as if he were about to argue, but she swept a hand toward the bathroom door. "You can wash up in there."

When Gray had disappeared, Andy looked up. "I'll stay, Ms. Mailer, if you want to go out. Anytime. You know that."

She smiled at him. "Thanks, Andy, but I don't think so. You work hard enough during the day. You deserve your time off. Besides, what about your girlfriend?"

He shrugged. "She could come over and help me. I mean, it's mostly just sitting around, isn't it? Maybe settling arguments if any come up, and there aren't so many guests that there's too much of that."

That, Donna had to admit ruefully, was the truth.

Gray came out a minute later, freshly scrubbed, her hair combed, his eyes seeking Donna immediately. She was setting a plate of sandwiches on the table, along with a bowl of salad.

"I'm baby-sitting the campers this evening, Gray," Andy said. "So you and Ms. Mailer can go catch a mess of fish for tomorrow's lunch."

"Andy! I said I didn't think so."

"Yeah, but you didn't say no. Come on, Ms. Mailer. I can use the overtime. College costs a bundle, you know."

Donna sighed and waved Gray to a chair. "I know. Okay, then. Thanks, Andy. Looks like we're on for fishing, Gray. Right after dinner." On impulse, she added, "To which you are invited. After all your hard work, the least I can do is feed you."

"Nope." He shook his head. "You work hard too. Why should you have to cook dinner? I'll bring a picnic."

She raised her brows as she picked up a wedge of tomato with her fork. "You can cook?"

He laughed. "Of course I can. I live alone, and even when I didn't, I did a lot of cooking. My mom made sure all her kids knew how to look after themselves. But this time," he added with a grin, "Maggie, my dad's housekeeper, will prepare the picnic. I won't have time, you see. I'll be busy brushing out the trail to the lake."

"Look," Donna said, tapping the bottom of the old yellow canoe. "I guess the manager and his family must have done something right. This thing's as sound as when I last saw it."

"Then let's go fishing," Gray said. He rolled the small craft over and slid it down a grassy bank and into the water. "We'll fish for . . . one hour?" She nodded in agreement, and he made a big production out of setting the alarm on his digital watch. "And whoever has the most fish at that time, wins."

"Right," she said. "Prepare to lose, Kincaid."

"We'll see." He steadied the canoe while she got in and then shoved off.

"We haven't established the stakes yet," she said, glancing back as they paddled away from the shore.

He looked down his nose at her. "You win, you get to kiss me. I win, I get to kiss you. Or would you rather go for something as mundane as mere cash?"

Something inside her quivered with need at the thought of the kisses they might be sharing soon, but she laughed and said, "Oh, I'm a terribly mundane person. And I love money! Think of all that overtime I have to pay Andy."

"'The love of money is the root of all evil,'" he said sanctimoniously.

"Hmm, yes. I know. Uncle Tyler used to say that frequently."

Gray grinned. "While he was failing to teach you to tie flies?"

"Exactly. I'm not a good student."

"All right, then, money, not kisses. How much money?"

"Ten?"

"Dollars or cents?"

She only grinned and faced the bow, slowing her paddle as they came to what she thought was a likely place to fish.

For a long time there was silence in their canoe as it bobbed on the surface of the lake, thirty feet from shore. Their orange lines lay on the placid water, lures near the shore where fish were likely to be hiding in the reeds. Donna jerked in a little line, teasing her unseen prey, making her fly appear to walk on the water. Then, letting out a small cry of triumph, she saw a swirl of water and felt a tug on her line.

In moments, she'd reeled in a ten-inch brown trout. She unhooked it and slipped it into the creel hanging over the side of the canoe.

She poked her thumb straight into the air, grinned at Gray, and cast again.

He laughed softly and splashed her with a few drops from the tips of his fingers.

A loon swam by, sweeping a bright eye over the humans. With a gentle brush of his hand on her bare arm, Gray drew Donna's attention to the bird. She nodded. A minute later he caught a fish, slightly larger than hers. By the time his alarm beeped, he had five and she had four.

He was a gracious winner, though, and didn't mention their bet.

"Dinner now," was all he said after they had beached the canoe and cleaned their fish, setting them in a cool, shady spot off the side of the trail. With the path now cleared, they shared the lake with several kids, some in canoes, one pair on an air mattress, and two swimming in the shallows under the watchful eyes of their mothers.

Gray looked at the much larger population than he'd anticipated, then shoved his way through the thick, hanging fronds of a weeping willow tree to a little cove where water lapped up against a narrow rim of sand.

Donna raised her brows as she hesitated halfway through the willow fronds. "Are you sure you've never been here before?"

"Never," he said, setting down the basket. "I spotted this place from out on the lake." He grinned. "Of course, seeing all those campers of yours follow us up the path, I was keeping an eye out for a likely spot."

She smiled, inordinately glad to hear him say that, whether it was true or not. This was, indeed, a "likely spot."

"But if you'd rather we had our picnic in sight of everyone else," he added, "that's fine with me too."

She let her hand fall and stepped into the bower with him. The willow branches fluttered as they settled back down behind her like a bamboo curtain.

Gray smiled.

Five

Unpacking the basket, Gray spread a small cloth on the ground, spooned potato salad onto two plates, added several crab legs to each, and a handful of cherry tomatoes.

Donna was impressed. "Your Maggie provides quite a picnic."

Gray patted his lean middle. "That's right. I normally gain at least five pounds during July, so eat up. Otherwise, I'll have to eat the leftovers for breakfast."

Leaning back against the trunk of the tree, Donna ate slowly, listening to the chatty goldfinches that populated the willow tree, watching swallows dip their wingtips into the lake surface, and drawing in the pungent aroma of Labrador tea growing around the shore. It was perfect there, idyllic, peaceful, and she was happy to share it in near silence with Gray Kincaid.

"I can't believe I'm doing this," she said when she accepted a second helping of everything from him. "It must be the fresh air."

"Or the hard work. Or," he added with a sly smile, "maybe I simply make you . . . hungry."

She threw a tomato at him. It bounced off his shoulder and fell into the lake with a splat. To their mutual amazement, a huge trout rose up in a swirl of water, striking at the tomato again and again before leaving with an angry splash of its tail, clearly disgruntled that the pretty morsel was more than he could manage.

They stared at each other in awed silence. "Want to try for that one?" Gray asked finally.

She shook her head. "Nope. That's a grand-daddy trout. It deserves to be left alone."

"Right." The smile he gave her told her he was pleased with her reply.

Finished at last, she lay flat on the ground, one arm tucked behind her head, her eyes closed. She was so stuffed, she thought she might never move again.

"You know," Gray said after several minutes of peaceful quiet, "you're a good person to be with, to fish with. You don't chatter unnecessarily."

Her eyes popped open and she stared at him, then she nodded serenely and closed her eyes again. "Neither do you. I appreciate that when I'm communing with nature."

"I'm a man!" he said, feigning indignation. "Men never chatter unnecessarily!"

Laughing, she rolled over to face him. "All your chatter is necessary, is it?"

He ran a fingertip from the tip of her shoulder to the crease of her elbow. "Of course. Man-talk is always more important than woman-talk. Don't you know anything about men?"

"Not a great deal," she confessed. But she wanted to know a lot more about this one. He looked so good lying there beside her, his long lean legs stretched out before him, his powerful shoulders pushed up as he rested on his elbows. The man looked as terrific in faded denims as he had in the business suit he'd worn the first day they met. She thought he'd look terrific even in coveralls—or nothing at all. He turned on his side, propped his head on a hand, and caressed her with his eyes.

"I realize it must have been tough, adjusting after your parents' death," he said. "But how did that make you a lonely child? I'd have thought, living in a campground, there'd have been plenty of kids for you to play with."

She shrugged in reply, and he said softly, "Come on, Donna, give a little. Didn't we paint that washroom to the tune of Gray Kincaid's childhood saga? I want to know about you."

She considered getting up and murmuring something about it being time to go home. She thought of closing her eyes quickly, pretending she was asleep and hadn't heard. If she rolled over once or twice, or maybe three or four times, she could join the big trout that lived under the bank, and make it look like an accident.

Something in his eyes, though, something more than just idle curiosity, kept her there, wondering how much to tell him. All he'd asked about was her childhood. That didn't mean she'd have to go on from there. After all, he knew about her time in Nova Scotia. Maybe he wouldn't notice the missing year.

He touched her cheek, the backs of his fingers gliding over the curve under her eye as if wiping away tears. She blinked. She was sure there had been none there.

"Were you like my brother," he asked gently, "not allowed to associate with the kids who came to the campground?"

"Of course I was allowed to. I was actively encouraged to. But it was hard."

His "Why?" was sympathetic. He genuinely cared, she realized.

"For one thing, coming from the prairies, I had culture shock to deal with as well as the loss of my parents. Up till then, I'd had a normal childhood in suburbia, living in a subdivision populated by young families with kids, so I was used to wall-to-wall playmates. Cordoba Island, and Clearwater Bay in particular, was like another world. A vastly underpopulated one. Everybody here knew about boats, and how a person's life had to be run around a ferry schedule. They knew about the tide coming in and going out, but to me, it was all completely alien. I was used to water that sat more or less at the same level. And the rain! There were some winters I actually cried from sheer relief when we got snow. Only, it never lasted for more than two or three days, so all the kids went wild while it was on the ground. The boys nearly killed everyone with snowballs all mixed up with grit and gravel, because it wasn't deep enough to be clean snow. But I got used to all that. I even came to like the mild winters, and of course it doesn't rain all winter. It just seems that way sometimes. What I couldn't adapt to was the isolation of living so far from town." She smiled wryly. "Not that 'town' is anything to speak of on Cordoba."

"I wish I'd known you were over here, and lonely," he said. "I'd have found a way to make it better for you."

She laughed as she shook her head. "Would you? It was odd enough, Jamie and I hanging around together, with four years separating us. For you and me, there'd have been an eight-year gap."

He went suddenly serious. "Is that too much?"

"My point is, it would have been then."

He sighed. "I guess you're right." Grinning, he added, "I'm glad we're adults now."

When she failed to comment on that, he said, "Well, go on. I still don't know why you were lonely, living in a place like this."

"I just didn't get close to the kids who came here. I played with them, but never really made friends."

He ran one finger through her hair, combing a lock to the front of her shoulder where he curled it around his thumb. "Why didn't you? In my experience, little girls usually make friends quickly." He laughed. "Trish often has a new best friend each time I see her."

"For me, it was the . . . impermanence of them," she said. "They came, they stayed a weekend, or a week or two, and then they were gone. They might come back next year, but they might not, so what was the point in getting close?"

"Of course." He slid closer and curved a hand around her jaw. His thumb caressed the skin below her ear. "But what about school? You had friends there, didn't you?"

"Oh, yes. But as I said, with the campground at the far end of the island from town, my social life was . . . limited."

"Right." His dimple flashed with his grin. "Like one sleep-over to last you an entire adolescence."

They both laughed, and she went on. "Of course, I saw my friends at school, but that was all. The quiet in the evenings, especially in winter, used to echo in my ears until it roared so loud I thought I would drown in it. I used to count off the days on my calendar until Jamie came back from boarding school so I'd have someone to talk to who understood what being alone really meant."

He shook his head ruefully. "And I used to yearn to have a room of my own, where I could study in peace. In a house where there weren't always four or five radios or tape decks competing, kids fighting, televisions blaring, dogs barking, and cats squabbling." He laughed softly. "I guess we never know when we're well off."

"I guess not." She certainly hadn't. She'd thought she knew what loneliness was, living with her aunt and uncle. Not until she had been sent away in disgrace, all but forbidden to return, had she known true isolation. She shivered. That was not something she wanted to think about.

"And then you left," he said. "What happened, Donna, to make you leave home so young?"

She shrugged and looked down at the ground, her fingers plucking nervously at the tiny pink and white daisies that dotted the grass. "When I was sixteen . . ." She paused, drew in a shuddering breath, and glanced at him. If he knew that Jamie had gotten a sixteen-year-old girl pregnant, and that she'd been sent away to have the baby in secret, now would be the time he put two and two together and figured out just how good the friendship between her and Jamie had been.

"What happened when you were sixteen?" he asked, his tone quiet, his gaze steady and level.

He didn't know! she thought. This final confirmation brought a great surge of relief.

"We had a . . . difference of opinion."

"Lifestyle?" he asked.

"Something like that." She continued plucking daisies. When she had a pile nearly two inches high, Gray reached out and stayed her hand.

"Leave some to enjoy next time we come," he said gently, and she stared at what she'd done.

"I'm sorry," she whispered.

"I'm sorry, too, for making you talk about something that you'd rather forget." He sat up and leaned his back on the tree. Spreading his legs wide, one on either side of her, he pulled her up between them to rest against his chest. "It can't have been easy, leaving home at that age, so vulnerable, so unprepared. And angry, too, I imagine." It was almost a question. She didn't mind his thinking she'd been a rebellious runaway.

"Oh, yes. I was angry. I thought I'd never want to come back, never want to see them again." She smiled. "But when Uncle Tyler said he needed me, in the most roundabout way possible, I remembered that when I'd needed them, they were there for me, had taken me in and cared for me, and I was almost a complete stranger to them. So I came back. Willingly." After her initial hesitation, she added silently, after a few weeks of fighting to overcome ten years' worth of distance on the part of her aunt and uncle, she had come back willingly.

"I'm glad of that," he said, sliding a hand up her throat. He cupped her chin and tilted her head back against his shoulder so he could see her face. "Do you have any idea just how glad, Donna? Since I met you, I've felt as if the world were all bright and shiny and new."

"Gray . . ." There was caution in her tone.

"What? Am I moving too fast for you?"

"I think so. I don't know. I like the world better, too, now that it has you in it, but we only met on Friday."

"And this is Wednesday. We spent most of yesterday together, all of today, and I hope we'll be together all of a lot more days." He slid his hands into her hair. "And from the moment you walked out of my office on Friday, even though I didn't see you, I thought of you constantly."

She sighed. "I sort of wondered if you'd call me over the weekend."

"And if I had?"

"I . . . don't know. I told myself I'd welcome the opportunity to tell you to get lost, but if it had come right down to it, I might not have."

"I wanted to call you, but I had other commitments."

A woman? She wanted badly to ask, but she knew she had no right to. She only looked at him, wondering if he'd feel the same way about her if he knew everything, wondering how he'd feel when he finally got around to telling his father where and with whom he was spending his time, and saw the reaction she knew was inevitable.

He smiled. "Hey, don't look so solemn. Haven't you enjoyed the time you've spent with me?"

"Yes," she said, then laughed. "Apart from the fact that you beat me at fishing."

"That's right. I did. Thanks for the reminder. I think you owe me ten dollars." His lips traced a line of fire along her jaw. "Or was it ten cents?"

She patted the pockets of her jeans. "Umm . . . I seem to be flat broke . . . just now," she said, trying to speak clearly through the heavy hammering in her throat.

"Broke maybe," he murmured as he slid his hands over the curves of her breasts in a strong and sensual motion that shocked her with its blatancy. "But not flat."

Her nipples peaked so sharply, they burned. Her breasts ached, her lower body heated and melted.

"I've been looking at your breasts all day," he said. "I've wanted to hold them in my hands." He did that, encircling them from below, lifting them, testing their weight. "I've wanted to suck on them." He sucked gently on an earlobe while tugging at her nipples. Then he kissed her earlobe and the side of her neck as he flattened both hands low on her abdomen and pressed gently.

"But if you haven't got ten cents . . ." he went on, turning her in his arms. He bent one leg behind her to act as a back rest as he drew her closer. "I'll settle for ten minutes."

As his mouth came down over hers, hard and warm and welcome, his tongue gliding along the seam of her lips, parting them, then plunging deep in short, rapid thrusts that set up a reciprocal pulsing deep inside her, she knew ten minutes would never be enough. Never.

"Donna," he said when he lifted his head, "I love the way you taste." He touched his lips to hers again, as if he couldn't get enough, either, then quickly broke the contact. "And I'd like to taste you a whole lot more, but those kids in the canoe out there might have parents who want them to get their sex ed in a different venue."

Donna glanced the way he was looking and laughed silently. Three boys of about ten, wearing fat orange life jackets, were bobbing in their craft twenty feet away, clearly interested in what was going on. She waved at them. After a startled, embarrassed moment at being caught watching, one of them lifted a hand in a halfhearted greeting, then they paddled quickly around the point and out of sight.

"Well!" Gray tumbled her back into his arms, laughing. "If I'd known it was that easy . . ."

"Never mind," she said. "There are sure to be others. Anyway, it's time to go."

He sighed. "If you say so."

On her front porch, after they'd said good night to Andy and watched him ride away on his bike, Gray slipped an arm around her waist. "Can I come and play again tomorrow?"

She wanted him to. She wanted it so much it scared her, and she forced herself to say no. "It's not a good idea, Gray. Besides, aren't you supposed to be spending your vacation with your father?"

He nuzzled the skin under her ear until she shivered and stepped away from him. "I'm not on vacation, remember? I quit my job. I'm unemployed."

"Then maybe I should put you on the payroll, if you insist on working for me. After all, you have a child to support."

He leaned on the rail, his expression sobering. "Yeah. That's something I've been meaning to talk to you about. My vacation—if I hadn't quit my job—would have officially started next Tuesday morning, right after the First of July long weekend." His mouth twisted wryly. "And the next month is not going to be easy, because I have a minor . . . complication, a problem seeing you, anyone, during July."

"I see." She pulled away from him abruptly. "Of course. I should have realized. When you're officially with your father, you wouldn't want to jeopardize your position as the reigning Kincaid son by dating me." She opened the door, prepared to step inside and shut him out. "Don't worry, Gray. If we should happen to run into each other, I promise not to expect any personal acknowledgment. I got used to that, you see, with your brother."

He gaped at her, astounded by what she was saying, but before he could cut in, she rushed on. "One thing I learned—the hard way—was that it wasn't to my advantage to sneak around and keep a friendship secret just because your father might disapprove. Either we're out of the closet, or we're not friends. Good night."

"Donna! What the hell is this all about?" He shouldered the door open and stood in the opening, staring down at her.

She tried to shove him out, but he wasn't budging.

"Just you wait one damn minute here," he said in a low, taut voice, fury sparking in his eyes as he snatched her to him again. "I don't give a damn what my father likes or dislikes, approves of or disapproves of, and I thought I'd made that clear. He has nothing to do with my not seeing you during July, and 'friends,' since you used the word, is not what I'm aiming for with you. I prefer the sound of the word 'lovers,' and I believe that's where we're headed."

She scowled at him, silent, until he let her go. "It takes two."

"I know that. I . . . Oh, hell, Donna, I don't want to fight with you. Please, let me explain."

"All right. Go ahead. Explain."

"It's because of my daughter, Trish. July is our month together, and I don't date when she's with me."

"I see."

He studied her. "No. No, I don't think you do. I think you see this as rejection, as my running out on you. But she was so broken up when her mother and I split up. Hell, you have no idea what promises that kind of guilt will drag out of a parent. And I promised her that our time together would be just that, ours. No . . . outsiders."

She met his gaze levelly. "I believe in keeping promises made, Gray. I wouldn't want to see you do anything else."

"But you're angry."

"No."

"Hurt?"

She shrugged. Of course she was! "I have no right to be hurt."

He traced a line from her temple to her chin, then around the sad curve of her mouth. "For the first time in three years, I find myself wishing I'd never made such a rash promise. But I did, Donna, and I don't know what to do."

His touch was unbearable at the moment. She slipped aside, putting some distance between them. "What to do, Gray, is honor your commitment to your daughter. I'm sure we can get together again. In August."

He stared at her. "August? Lord almighty, woman! Do you think I want to—or intend to—wait until August? I want you now, and I'll want you tomorrow and the day after, and the day after and—" He broke off and ran a hand through his hair, then leaned against the door, closing it. "What I'm saying is that we have two more days before Trish arrives on Saturday, and I want to spend all that time with you."

"I have to work."

"I know you do. So I want to work with you. Just . . . don't shut me out, okay? Let me be as big a part of your life as I can. Because—"

"Because as of Saturday, you won't be any part of my life, right?"

"No." He slumped back against the door, shaking his head. "No, of course not." He sighed, then brightened. "Listen . . . My father always has a big party for business associates and friends every year on the July first long weekend. Saturday night we have fireworks. You could come to that. You could—You could . . . meet Trish, sort of in a casual way, a way that wouldn't make her feel threatened."

She searched his face. "You want me to meet your daughter while I'm disguised as one of your father's business associates."

She wondered if he knew this was the first time she had ever received an invitation to Chester Kincaid's home. She wondered what Chester would say if he knew Gray was inviting her. Donna would have laughed if she could. Oh, yes, there'd be fireworks, all right, if she showed up at Chester Kincaid's house!

"Sort of," she went on, "sneak around without giving the appearance of sneaking around?"

"No! Dammit, no."

"Then what, Gray? How would you introduce me? If you said I was your 'friend,' wouldn't that upset her?"

He looked miserable as he headed for a chair and sat down, elbows on his knees, chin on one hand, looking at her pleadingly. "Yes. No. Probably. Oh, hell, I don't know! Can't we wait until then and see how things look and feel to us?"

Quickly she opened the door again. After a moment's hesitation Gray got the message, and stood and walked over to her. He looked at her searchingly, then bent and kissed her, long and hard, then he was gone.

• • •

"Let me do that," Gray said, startling Donna. It was only seven o'clock Thursday morning and she hadn't been expecting him, not that early, maybe not at all. With a look of total exasperation on his face as she stubbornly hung on to the barrel she was manhandling into the back of a pickup truck, he hefted it up for her. Before she could protest, he snatched her thick leather gloves off her hands and shoved his own into them. Fortunately, the only gloves she'd been able to find were men's large, and they fit him. He heaved another heavy garbage can into the back of the truck with the others she'd already managed to load, as she wrestled with an empty one from the other side of the truck.

"Where's Andy?" he asked as she got behind the wheel and he slid into the passenger seat of the pickup. "You shouldn't be doing this."

"It's his day off."

Gray snorted.

"Hey, come on. The kid's entitled to a couple of days off a week, you know."

"I know, I know. It's just that I hate to see you doing this kind of stuff. What about your part-time kids?"

"Jennifer's cleaning out the coin laundry, and Majumdar's splitting wood." She backed up to the next large oil drum used for garbage disposal and opened her door. "If you don't like to see me doing work like this, you don't have to come here. If I were on vacation, believe me, seven A.M. would be before breakfast for me!"

"I'm not on vacation, remember? I'm unemployed."

"Gray, please, don't play games. I don't have time for it."

His hand clamped on her arm as he pulled her

around to face him. "Hey, now. Last night you said that I could come and play at your house today. So let's pretend. Let's pretend you're the driver and I'm the swamper." Before she could respond, he grabbed the leather gloves again, leaped out, and lifted the big can easily into the back of the truck. He replaced it with a clean one, then they were on their way again.

"See how well this works?" he said after the fourth exchange had been made. "See what a little cooperation can accomplish?"

"It seems to me," Donna said, "that you're the only one accomplishing anything, the only one doing any work. Gray, I hate feeling useless. I'm not a weakling. This is a job I've been doing every day since Monday and I managed fine up to now."

There was no need to add, she told herself, that Andy had acted as swamper on all but the first of those days, and that day, Monday, she'd been so filled with the adrenaline of fury, she could have lifted mountains. She had to make a point here, that she was capable of running her campground on her own. Whatever help Gray wanted to offer she would take, but she didn't want him to think she was relying on him.

She didn't want to let herself think that she could rely on him. After this coming weekend, she might not see him again.

Was it her lot in life, she wondered as they drove in silence toward the landfill site halfway across Cordoba Island, to fall in love with Kincaid men who wanted to keep her hidden from their nearest and dearest? First Jamie with his parents, and now Gray with his daughter. It didn't seem fair and—

"Watch it!"

Gray's sharp words corrected her wandering

steering, and she gripped the wheel much too tightly. *Fall in love?* Was that what she was doing? Falling in love? With Gray Kincaid?

"Are you all right?" he asked. "You look pale. Is something wrong?"

"Wrong?" She laughed, wondering if what she felt, this terrible confusion of emotions, everything mixed in and churning, halfway between laughter and tears, was the beginnings of hysteria. "No. Nothing's wrong." Oh, Lord! Everything was wrong! What had she done? How much more badly could she screw up her life without even trying? Fall in love with Gray Kincaid? The stupidity of it appalled her.

For more years than she liked to remember, she hadn't even come close to falling in love. Now she'd done it in less than a week with the man most unlikely in all the world to be able to return her feelings with a clear conscience. And if, by some crazy miracle, he did, the minute she told him about the past, his feelings would surely change.

"Donna!"

"Oh!" She snatched the truck back toward the center of the road, eyes widening at the sight of the ditch much too close to her right front wheel. "Sorry."

"Donna, do you want me to drive?"

"No." With difficulty, she focused her attention on negotiating the narrow, washboard gravel road. "I'm fine. Really. I was just . . . thinking."

"What about?"

She flicked a glance at him. "Gray! People are allowed to keep some of their thoughts private, you know."

He grinned, looking extremely masculine and greatly smug. "Good," he said. "When a woman refuses to tell a man her thoughts, chances are she's been thinking about him."

Donna bumped the truck to a stop and backed into a spot where it would be easy to empty the drums. "Quite the expert, aren't you?"

He sat there for another moment or two, not looking at her, but at the sea gulls that wheeled and screamed around the refuse. A pair of bald eagles landed heavily, one ahead of the other, on a craggy limb, scaring up a black shower of crows.

"I'm no expert, Donna," he said slowly. "Not about you." He turned to face her. "But I'd like to be."

She met his gaze, searched it, saw nothing she could understand. "Can one person ever be an expert about another?"

He was thoughtful. "Maybe not. But two people can grow close enough that each is able to figure out what the other wants and needs, often without being told. I saw that with my mom and stepfather. When my own marriage didn't work that way, I envied them and spent a lot of time analyzing, trying to figure out where Sheila and I went wrong."

"Did you?" she asked, wondering about the sanity of having an important discussion in a garbage dump. "Did you ever figure it out?"

"I think so. We didn't do much together after we got married. She didn't like my friends. I didn't like her friends. We both had jobs that kept us busy. When we got home in the evening, we were often too tired to cook a meal together, let alone sit down and eat it together and talk. And we both normally brought work home, so she'd go into our bedroom to her desk, and I'd stay in the living room at mine. What we were, after the first year or so, were roommates who sometimes made love if we both had the time and the inclination, and who were trying to raise a child together. Once we realized it wasn't going to be any different, no matter how long we stayed together, we parted."

Donna didn't quite know what to say. "I'm sorry."

"So am I. And I feel a large part of it was my fault, because I thought, having been raised by two people who communicated freely, argued openly, and resolved their differences in whatever novel way suited them, that it would happen the same way for Sheila and myself without any effort on our part. I was wrong."

He reached across the cab of the truck and stroked a finger down her cheek. "I don't want to make the same kind of mistakes again, Donna." His gaze held hers, and she knew what he was asking of her. But this was scary! It was more than scary. It was downright terrifying. She had never shared much of herself with anyone. But, she had to wonder, was that simply because she'd never had anyone with whom to share?

Did she have the courage to try? With Gray? She drew in a long breath and let it out slowly. "All right. I *was* thinking about you."

"Good. Because I was thinking about you. I've spent every waking minute and quite a few sleeping ones since last Friday with you right smack in the center of my mind. What were you thinking?"

"That—that I shouldn't learn to rely on you to be here to help me with the hard things, because I know it's not possible for it to continue. Because, come the weekend, your little girl will be with you and then you won't be spending any more time with me."

He curled his hand behind the back of her head. "I won't be spending all of my time with you," he said. "But I intend to be with you as much as I can." His eyes searched hers. "I've decided it's time to tell Trish that Daddy has a lady who is very, very important to him, and she'll have to learn to adjust."

Donna's breath caught in her throat, making her voice come out choppy. "Gray . . . Don't upset your daughter on my account. Please! You mustn't do that."

He unclipped her seat belt and slid her out from behind the wheel, pulling her tightly against him. "Why? Why not?" He frowned. "Dammit, are you involved with someone back east or something?"

"No! No, of course not. What do you think I am? If I were in a relationship with another man, I wouldn't have been doing with you, what . . . uh, what I've been doing."

He grinned. "You mean this?"

She was weak with desire when his mouth finally released hers. He passed a hard thumb over her moist and tender bottom lip. "Lord!" he said, breathing hard. "Great Lord almighty. Your kisses do something really extraordinary to me, Donna Mailer. What am I going to do?"

She slipped back behind the wheel, gripping it with hands that shook so hard, she wondered if she'd be able to drive. "Dump the garbage?" she suggested in a small voice.

He grinned and pulled on the heavy leather gloves again. "Right," he said. "That's what I love about you. You're always so practical."

Before she could even begin to formulate a reply, he was out of the truck and clanking the heavy barrels as he lifted them out of the truck and heaved their contents.

Donna turned on the ancient radio and kept it loud enough to preclude conversation on the way back to their end of the island, but she didn't hear a word the phone-in host or his callers said. Her mind was whirling, dancing, settling for a second and then sailing off on another tangent, like the clouds of sea gulls that spun out their lives over the landfill—and with about as much intelligent thought.

That's what I love about you. . . .

Was it the same as saying "That's what I love about ice cream, it's so sweet?" Or "That's what I love about politics, it's so interesting"?

Or was it like saying "That's what I love about you, that fact that I find you worthy of my love"?

She wanted, desperately, to know, but was much too afraid to ask.

Six

"Ms. Mailer! Ms. Mailer!" Majumdar's voice was shrill with panic. "Come quick! Hurry!"

Donna, followed by Gray, flew from the house, where they'd just finished washing up after their garbage detail. "What's wrong?"

"It's the little Moberg boy, hornets got him. Lots of hornets. Oh, he's really stung bad." As he talked, Majumdar led them at a run along one of the paths to where a family of four was camped. They stood in a huddle of other people in an adjacent site, many of whom were offering loud and conflicting suggestions as to how to treat the little boy.

"What happened?" Donna asked, shouldering her way through the crowd. She halted beside the table where the hurt child stood, being attended by his mother. "Marilyn . . . Oh, Lord, poor Michael!" The child had at least ten stings on his arms and legs, and three on his face. "Where was the nest?" she asked. "Did you see where he was when he got stung?"

Marilyn, whom Donna had first met when the

two of them were thirteen years old, didn't even look up from dabbing soothing ointment on her son's injuries. "Right under our damned picnic table!" she snapped. "That's where the nest was! How could you let something like that happen, Donna? No hornets would have had a chance to build their nest there when your uncle was in charge."

"Marilyn, believe me, I can't tell you how sorry I am. The rest of your stay will be on the house, of course, and I'll make absolutely certain there isn't a hornet's nest within a mile of the area."

"The rest of our stay will be somewhere else," said Marilyn's husband. "When you get him finished, honey, put him in the camper. Larraine's there now, where she's safe. I've got everything stowed. We'll be ready to roll as soon as I get the boat out of the water." He shot Donna a poisonous look and strode away.

"They'll never come back," Donna said sadly, watching the Mobergs drive off. She wandered disconsolately into the house and slumped on the comfortable old sofa Aunt Sadie had always kept at one end of the kitchen. "Marilyn used to come here with her mom and dad. As a matter of fact, her parents and another couple are booked in for the last two weeks of July. I bet they'll cancel after this." She pounded the arm of the couch, releasing a small cloud of dust with each whap of her fist. "Damn, damn, damn! Why didn't I do a proper check?"

Gray sat beside her and captured her hand, holding it tightly so she couldn't hammer the couch. "Donna, quit beating yourself with it, will you?" he said impatiently. "How many people have used that site since hornet season began? And how many complained that there were more hornets around than usual? None, right? So how could you have known you should check the underside of the table and see if anything was hatching there?"

"I should have thought of it."

"You have been here less than four days and you've been working steadily since you arrived. How can you expect yourself to have thought of every little detail and anticipated every problem? You are, I believe, human?"

"Yes. Yes, of course, but I just feel sick over a little kid getting hurt because I overlooked something I might have seen, if only I'd been looking."

"Well, we've checked every other site and found nothing, so that's one less thing you have to worry about. It's just plain bad luck the little Moberg kid chose to play hide and seek with his sister and climbed under the table, but it is not your fault."

Donna knew he was right, but it didn't help. She was responsible. A little child was hurt, his parents were angry, and the business had suffered just one more piece of damage. It was all those little pieces that added up, and she wished she knew how to avoid the possibility of other things going wrong.

"You know what I think you need?" Gray asked.

She gave him a rueful glance. "Not food. I ate breakfast and it's scarcely ten, so don't go telling me I'm cranky because my blood sugar's low."

He laughed. "No. Not food. A swim, then a nice long soak in the Jacuzzi, followed by another dip in the pool. What do you say? Feel like playing hookey for a couple of hours? If Andy gets two days off a week, you should at least allow yourself a few hours."

She stared at him as if he were crazy. For a moment she thought of accusing him of being just that. But no, he wasn't nuts. He simply didn't understand. He was clearly accustomed to being able to walk away from his responsibilities when the going got tough, just as Jamie had done. It wasn't Gray's fault he'd become used to having enough money to take the easy way out. It was just the way it was. She shook her head and stood. There was work to be done, plenty of it, and no time for swimming and lolling in a hot tub. Especially considering where that pool and Jacuzzi were located.

"No," she said gently. "But thanks anyway."

He stood too. "Because the pool and Jacuzzi are at my father's place?"

She shrugged. "Your asking that tells me you already know the answer."

He nodded. "My friends are always welcome in my father's home, Donna. Because if they aren't, he knows I'll stop going there."

She thought about that for a minute, then shook her head again. She had to be honest with herself. Her plans to reopen the small convenience store at the back of the house wouldn't see fruition that day, whether she declined to take a couple of hours off or not. And if she was being honest with herself, why not be honest with Gray? That was what he'd been talking about an hour or so ago, wasn't it? Being open with each other? Communicating freely?

"I don't want to become a bone of contention between you and your father," she said. "I'm sure he's angry enough, knowing you're spending all your time over here with me. Why aggravate him further?"

Gray hesitated before answering. The fact was,

he still had not told his father where he was spending his days, or with whom. Not that Chester had asked. Since Gray had quit his job, Chester had little to say to him. Gray knew his father was waiting for him to make the first move, but that was not something he intended to do. Chester had gone too far, paying the manager to leave Tyler French in the lurch.

He wondered if he'd be as angry if it really had been Tyler who'd been hurt by his father's actions, instead of Donna. He hoped his outrage would be the same no matter who his father had tried to cheat.

He looked at Donna. "He doesn't know where I spend my time. And he knows better than to ask."

She shook her head as she smiled quizzically at him. "You know, I can't believe how different you are from Jamie."

"Don't forget, you knew Jamie when you were a kid. When he was a kid." He tapped his chest with two fingers. "Me? Lady, I'm a *man*."

She laughed softly. "I've noticed."

Crowding in close, he pressed his body against hers. "Have you, now?" He slipped his arms around her waist, as she slid hers around his neck. "And, having noticed, what do you plan to do about it?"

"Gray . . ." She trailed her lips along his jaw-line, unable to resist the slightly sandpapery texture of his chin. "I don't know. Honestly, I just don't know."

"I know what I plan to do about the fact that I've noticed you're a woman," he said gruffly. He cupped her buttocks and rocked her forward against the hard, rigid line of his sex. "The question is, when?"

"That's . . . that's something else I don't know," she whispered through a tight throat.

"But soon," he said, and she knew it wasn't a question.

They worked together—and apart—for the rest of the day, then separated just before dinner, Donna pleading exhaustion and the need for an early night.

Yet for all that, she lay awake long after retiring, thinking about Gray, wondering at the amazing depth of her newly discovered love, and wondering where it would end. She much preferred books with happy endings. Indeed, she refused to read anything else. But real life? That, she knew, was an entirely different thing. Experience had taught her that happy endings were more likely to be found in fiction than in fact.

"But just this once?" she whispered into the dark. "Just this once, couldn't I have one? Please?"

Friday evening Donna cooked dinner for Gray despite his protests that she'd done enough for one day.

"Besides," he'd added, "if we go out, you won't have to be answering the door every five minutes so someone can buy something in the convenience store. You were crazy to reopen it. They've been flocking in there all day as if they were hoarding in case of disaster."

Donna had nodded happily. "Just goes to show what a need there is for the store. And I put up a Closed sign as soon as Majumdar went off duty. I intend to stick to the hours I have posted. That's the way Aunt Sadie did it, and people respected her time off. She simply and graciously refused to let them do otherwise."

Donna baked potatoes in the microwave and tossed a salad while Gray barbecued the steaks he'd bought on the rusty old hibachi she'd unearthed in the shed.

"You did a good job, getting that store up and running as fast as you did," he said when they had finished eating and were sitting on the front porch swing. Donna had thrown a blanket over it to hide the split cushions and decided to keep it. Maybe someday soon she could replace the padding.

"When I found those boxes of T-shirts and silver spoons and other souvenir items all neatly stored away, it seemed silly to delay. All of that stuff was already paid for, so what I get for it now just adds to the cash flow without costing me anything but Jennifer's and Majumdar's wages. And both kids are glad to have full-time summer work."

"I hate the idea of your having to buy those grocery items you stocked at retail price, though," he said.

"I marked them up. People expect to pay a bit more for the convenience of not having to drive all the way into town when they need a can of tomato soup or a half pound of butter, or the kids want pop. When I have time, I'll set up an account with the wholesaler my uncle used to deal with."

Assuming, she didn't add, that the manager hadn't managed to alienate that company too. She didn't think so, because as far as she could tell, he and his family had never opened the store for the convenience of the guests. She'd been forced to throw away several cases full of rusty canned goods, and that had pained and angered her.

In peaceful silence she and Gray watched the light fade. When she sighed, then yawned, he drew her into his arms and put her head on his shoulder, stroking her hair.

"I should go home, shouldn't I?" he murmured. "You're tired and need to get some sleep."

She didn't argue, just turned her face to his and pulled his head down for a good-night kiss. And then another . . . and another.

Their kisses grew long and deep, but instead of satisfying her, they set up a pulsating desire in Donna that she felt through her whole body, a need for more, a yearning for his touch all over. As if he knew what she longed for, he pulled her half onto his lap and curved a hand under one breast, lifting it as he had that day at the lake. This time, though, he bent his head, his breath hot and moist through her T-shirt, and opened his mouth over her. When his lips closed on the taut nipple, his teeth nipping gently, she sucked in a sharp, shaken breath, arching up to him.

Slowly, watching her eyes in the dim light, he slid his hand under her top. He smiled when her abdominal muscles quivered, then sobered when he felt her breast swell and grow warm against his palm. "Oh, sweetheart, you feel good," he said raggedly. "Such a beautiful shape!" He stroked a thumb over the hard nipple. "So responsive."

She tangled her hands in his thick hair and pulled his head down, needing his lips on hers. She opened her mouth for his tongue, tasting him, feeling the hard thrust of his erection as he pulled her higher against him. In moments, even the thin satin of her bra was too great a barrier, and she murmured, "Touch me, Gray. My skin . . ."

He fumbled with her bra. "Where does this damn thing fasten?" he muttered. "Front or back?"

She tingled all over. Her blood felt thick. Her throat was so tight from holding back the need to moan, it was all she could do to reply, "Back . . ."

His hand slid around her ribs, following the line

of her bra, and his fingers worked deftly for a second unhooking it. As he pushed it up, she murmured his name, feeling his hand, hard and callused, abrading the soft underside of her breast.

"I need to suck on you," he said hoarsely, staring into her eyes, his own nothing but a faint silvery gleam between his thick lashes. "To feel you hot and hard in my mouth. To taste you."

With trembling hands, she pulled her T-shirt up, baring her breasts for him. His gaze slid from her face to the wrinkled fabric of her T-shirt, and downward. He tilted her back. She felt his trembling sigh as it escaped from his chest, but though he had expressed a need, he didn't immediately fulfill it. Instead, he caressed her lightly, fingertips inscribing circles from the outside inward, not quite touching her nipples, until both her breasts burned with the need for more.

He held one, lifted it, squeezed gently, and then slowly, so slowly she thought she'd go mad with the waiting, he bent toward it and touched her nipple with the tip of his tongue. He held it there forever, applying a light, rhythmic pressure, as gentle as a butterfly's touch, until she sobbed aloud and thrust herself into his mouth.

He sucked. Hard. Deep. His hand massaged her other breast. His breath grew hotter and hotter, making her melt, turning her to liquid fire as she held his head to her.

She needed desperately to turn, to straddle him, to take his hardness into her, to fill herself with it, with him, and assuage the ache deep inside her. He held her fast, though, and when he moved from one breast to the other and she felt the cool air after the heat of his mouth, the contrast sent a deep, sensual shudder through her.

"Gray . . . Gray . . ." She heard her own voice pleading from a long way off.

He groaned, then tore his mouth from her breast. He refastened her bra, pulled her shirt down, and leaned his head back, gasping, shaking, swallowing hard. She heard his rough breathing, smelled the musk of his overheated skin. He reached out and cradled her against him, his hands running over her arms, her face, her back, trembling and hard.

"Oh, Lord, how I want you," he whispered after several moments. "Donna . . . I want to be inside you right now. I want to lay you down and press your legs apart and slide myself into you where you're hot and wet and tight."

"Oh, please, don't!" It was all she could do to speak. How had a few good-night kisses escalated to such passion so fast? Was it because he spoke to her in such blunt terms, as no one ever had before? She found it wildly thrilling, erotic, as physically exciting as any kiss or caress.

She lifted her head and looked into his eyes. "Don't say those things to me, because—because I want all of that too," she whispered shyly, half afraid he meant to do it right then, half afraid he didn't.

"I know," he said, pulling her back into his embrace. "I know, love."

Love? Did he mean that as only a simple endearment? Moments passed. When she finally moved apart from him, Gray took her left hand and tucked it into the crook of his neck, lowering his head to pin her fingers against his warm skin. He smiled into her eyes.

"I think I've got it real bad, Ms. Mailer. For the first time in a long while, I'm finding it harder to say good night than I did when I was a horny eighteen-year-old. I'm not, as I've become accustomed to doing, looking forward to my privacy tonight, my solitude, the room to sprawl across the entire bed. Since I met you, privacy feels more like loneliness after I've said good night."

She traced the straight line of his eyebrows as she drew a deep, unsteady breath. "Then . . . don't."

"Don't what?"

"Don't say good night."

His eyes glittered as he shook his head, laughing softly. "Hey, you. Be careful what you say to a badly stirred up male beast."

She cradled his face in her hands, her fingers trembling, her mouth close to his. "Gray, I know what I'm saying. I want you too. Come inside with me."

He stared at her, covering her hands with his. "Do you mean it?"

"Yes." She slipped her hands free and stood, then looked down at him. "Come in with me. Make love with me."

He rose swiftly, reaching out for her, then held back. "Are you sure, Donna?"

She nodded, unable to speak for the thickness in her throat. Was he going to reject her? She felt sick, dizzy. She loved him, but did he love her? She knew he wanted her. That was something he couldn't hide, couldn't be ambivalent about. But love? Twice he had used the word, and she still had no idea what it meant to him.

"I'll have to go out to my car for a minute," he said, and again she nodded.

When he returned, they shared a smile and he took her hand, walking into her house with her, into her bedroom. A small lamp burned by her bed. In its light, he feasted his eyes on her taut nipples, clearly visible through her shirt. Then he asked her again.

"Are you sure? Donna, believe me, I'm no saint, but if you want to change your mind, I'll understand. I won't make trouble. I know sometimes we say things we might mean at that exact moment, when things are, well, hot and heavy, but on the walk into the house, you . . . any woman . . . might change her mind."

For an answer, she pulled her T-shirt off and walked into his waiting arms.

"Oh, Lord, woman, I want you," he said, his voice a low growl. His mouth trailed along the line of her jaw until he found the tender patch of skin below her ear. He nuzzled there as he unfastened her bra again, slipped it off her, and drew her tightly against him. The cotton of his shirt rubbed against her bare breasts, stroking her nipples to greater sensitivity. She shivered with pleasure and smiled at him.

He kissed her cheeks, her eyebrows, her ears. "Ever since I met you, all I've been able to think of is this. I wanted to lie down with you, on you." He lifted her and laid her gently on the bed, then shifted his weight so he half covered her. "In you!"

She moaned softly, clinging to him, sliding one bent knee the length of his thigh, feeling the hardness of his muscles through his soft, faded jeans. She pulled his shirt free and stroked her hands up his back, so filled with need she could scarcely breathe. "I've wanted you, too, from the very beginning."

Quickly, he stood and stripped, dropping his clothes on the floor. Then he knelt beside her, unsnapping her jeans and sliding the zipper down. His fingers trailed over her taut belly, his lips following. She lifted her hips, and he drew her pants off her, then ran a finger around the lacy elastic of her bikini panties. "Satin," he said, and slid his fingers inside, raking his nails lightly through the rusty patch of hair. "And silk."

She slid her hand down his thigh, feeling hard muscles, warm skin, and rough hair. She delighted in the contrasting textures, in the way his muscles quivered as he knelt beside her, the way his eyes glittered as he watched her hand track all the way back up. He caught it and pressed it where he wanted it, holding it there, moving it up and down, his eyes never leaving hers.

"Iron," she whispered. "And velvet."

"Oh, God . . ." He thrust into her palm, and she stroked him again from root to tip until he snatched her hand away and buried his face against her breasts.

She shuddered with pleasure, closing her eyes. "Kiss me," she said.

He lay on his side with her head on one arm and kissed her gently, then deeply, then gently again, running the tip of his tongue over her lips. She caressed his chest, fingers stroking in ever smaller arcs. She found his hard nipples and teased them, then kissed one while she tugged on the other. He moaned and rolled so that she was on top of him, and raked his nails down her back, over her buttocks, making her arch her hips into his.

His sex was a hard, hot rod pressing her belly, and she burned with need. Writhing on top of him, she plunged her tongue wildly into his mouth. Her soft cries of arousal incited him until he slid away, readied himself, and came back to her.

As he slid between her legs, she drew her knees up, making a cradle for him. Her hips lifted in an erotic rhythm that aroused him almost beyond reason but he didn't want to rush this. It was too beautiful, too special, too incredible. Yet try as he did to hold her still, he couldn't stem the desire for completion as she thrust her hips upward to take him in. He closed his eyes and plunged deep, lifted and plunged again, again, listening to the hungry moans that his loving brought from her throat. He opened his eyes and watched as a rosy flush rose over her breasts, onto her cheeks. He felt her muscles begin their spasms, saw it in her eyes as her climax came in a rushing, roaring deluge and she flung her head back, calling his name on a long sigh of ecstasy.

"Sweetheart!" he cried. "Donna!" He thrust with one last, deep stroke that carried him to where she had already sailed.

"Donna?" he said presently as his strength began to return. "I have to move now, love. We wouldn't want any accidents."

She opened her eyes slowly, smiled at him, and helped him withdraw carefully, so there would be no accidents. She loved him for his care, for his tenderness. She loved him.

They showered together, nuzzling, laughing, playing like wet puppies, and when they went back into the bedroom, they snuggled together under the sheet.

Half an hour later Donna felt Gray slide his arms from around her, easing away, trying not to disturb her.

"Don't go," she murmured, only half awake.

His lips brushed her cheek. "I have to, sweetheart. I wouldn't want to embarrass you by leaving after daylight, and if I stay, I'll fall asleep."

She turned her face and found his lips with hers. "I wouldn't be embarrassed. Stay if you want to."

"Kiss me like that again, and I won't be able to leave."

She laughed softly against his throat. "Didn't I see you take two little packages out of the car?" she asked slyly, and kissed him like that again. He didn't need a second invitation.

It was the sound of several outboard motors winding up that woke them as daylight came.

Gray lifted himself on one elbow and smiled down at her. "Hi," he said. "How are you?"

"I'm fine. How about you?"

His smile was slow and wide. "I," he said expansively, "have never felt better in my entire life." He poked his nose against that spot under her ear and breathed hotly against it, then inhaled. "You smell good, love." He licked her. "You taste good too."

Her nipples popped out, demanding attention, attention he willingly offered. Finally, although she was shuddering with pleasure, she pushed him away. "Enough. Stop now, or I'll lose my head."

His chuckle was warm and rumbly. "If we don't stop now, I'll lose more than my head." Rolling onto his back and bringing her with him, he said, "Let me lose it, Donna. In you."

She closed her eyes. "No. Like you said last night, no accidents, Gray. Unless you want to make another trip out to your car?"

He tumbled her back onto her own pillow. "I would, but it would mean making another trip to the drugstore. I don't run around with a gross of those things in my glove compartment, you know."

She angled herself up on one elbow. "No? Why not? No confidence, Kincaid?"

Groaning, he dragged her into his arms. "You give me confidence, lady. You give me enough confidence to say something I haven't said for a long, long time." He tilted her back and looked directly into her eyes. "I love you, Donna Mailer, and if I were to make a baby in you, I wouldn't look upon it as an accident, but as a blessing from heaven."

Before she could so much as draw a startled breath, he shot out of her bed, grabbed his clothes, and headed for the shower.

When he came back, she was waiting for him, wrapped tightly in her robe, wrapped tightly in self-control, wrapped tightly in misery.

He sat beside her on the bed. "What's wrong, sweetheart? Didn't you want me to fall in love with you?"

She shook her head. "And I didn't want to fall in love with you, either, Gray."

"Did you?" He cradled her face. "Do you?"

"I love you," she said, and blinked back tears.

He kissed her lightly, his eyes somber. "Love is supposed to make people happy. Why is it making you so miserable?"

She knew she should explain. She knew what kind of relationship he was looking for: one where neither held anything back from the other. But if she was completely open, she'd have to admit that she had once borne his half brother's baby, once been Jamie's lover for the length of a summer, and was scared to death that that was all she was destined to be to Gray—a summer lover. She should tell him how afraid she was of his father, of his daughter, and their positions in his life, so much more solid than hers could ever be. But she couldn't. All she could do was cling to him and tell him how much she loved him.

"Sweetheart . . . I have to go now," he said several minutes later. "I need to go home and change, then take the ferry over to get Trish. It's amazing the amount of luggage one little girl needs for a month during which she wears hardly anything but swimsuits. I have a suspicion it has something to do with her being female."

She nodded and stood, managing a credible smile. "Watch it, buster! I'm female, in case you haven't noticed, and I refuse to let you malign my sex."

He laughed. "Honey, there ain't a thing wrong with your sex," he said, with a slight emphasis on the pronoun, "and I most certainly did notice that you are female."

He held her tightly, running his hands up and down her back, pressing her to him. "Oh, Lord, but it's hard to leave you!" He tilted her face up. "Come with me, Donna. Come with me to get Trish."

Her eyes widened at the suggestion. "No! Not on your life! Even if I didn't have a thousand things to do here today, I wouldn't intrude on your time with your daughter."

"Why not?" he asked. He sounded almost sullen, and for the first time she saw just a hint of resemblance to Jamie. "Why not?" he asked again. "She's going to be intruding on my time with you."

"Gray . . ." Slipping a hand behind his neck, she pulled his face down and kissed him tenderly. "Trish has first priority. You made her a promise a long time ago. I'd hate to have you break that promise on my behalf."

"It's going to have to be broken sometime."

"Maybe. But not until she's had a chance to get used to the idea of . . . sharing."

He sighed. "I know you're right, but dammit, I

feel like I'm being torn right now, wanting to be two people, wanting to be in two places, wanting . . ." He let his voice trail off and shook his head.

"Wanting?"

He laughed. "You!" Taking her hand, he placed it on his body so she'd know just how much he wanted her. The sensation of her touching him, even through his jeans, was so exquisite, he closed his eyes. "I'll be having that little talk with Trish soon, Donna. Likely before tonight."

As Donna watched him drive away, she ached with need and wondered if tonight would ever happen. Something very basic in her doubted it. Because, of course, if Gray told his daughter who he'd fallen in love with, he'd have to tell his father too. Then, she knew, he'd learn all the things she should have told him herself, but hadn't, out of pure, yellow cowardice.

Tonight, she promised herself. If there was a tonight, she'd tell him. She would. She would . . .

Seven

"I'll simply keep too busy to think about him," Donna said to herself as she forced down a few bites of breakfast. The thought that she might not see Gray that day, or even the next day, was too much to bear.

She worked hard all morning, doing garbage duty with Andy, then spelling Jennifer in the campground store for half an hour. She had to restrain herself from running out onto the front porch every time she heard a car go by. It wouldn't be Gray. She knew that. But oh, how she wanted it to be!

Finally, in mid-afternoon, she knew she had to get away from the house. She mounted the old ride-on mower, running it across the orchard Andy had mowed on Wednesday and out into the meadow beyond, where she knew mosquitoes still bred unchecked. She had avoided the meadow until now because it was there, at the edge of the forest, she and Jamie had met, had built their treehouse—and their dreams.

Maybe, she thought, it was time she visited the

place and proved to her own satisfaction that over the past decade it had rotted and crumbled and fallen, as their dreams had. It was time to put the past to rest. In doing that, she might dare to reach out for the future.

Her future, and Gray's.

She stopped the mower and shut off the motor to enjoy the silence.

There it was, the old maple, in full and glorious leaf. This time of year, the treehouse, if any of it remained, would be all but invisible.

She dismounted and waded through high brush toward the tree, halting when a flash of blue near its trunk caught her eye. Suddenly, her heart hammered hard in her chest. Was someone there? Moments later a skirling squeak sounded, and she frowned. Her breath caught in her throat, until she laughed at herself and moved onward.

It had been a bird she'd seen in that brief flash of color. A Stellar's jay. Jays were well known for their variety of calls, including mimicking rusty hinges. Of course there was no one in the treehouse. No one had pushed up the trap door in the floor and entered from below. If the treehouse had occupants, they lived only in her memory. Ghosts.

She had nearly reached the trunk of the tree, intent on convincing herself that not even the old ladder remained after all this time, when more sounds startled her. From just beyond the fence she heard running footsteps on the dusty road, and the honking of a car horn. She spun around, peering through the tall bracken.

A woman, huffing, puffing, and wheezing, trundled past Donna, her face red, her gray hair awry, her plump arms and breasts jiggling as she ran. A car came after her, a plume of dust curling up behind it, horn still honking madly. Before Donna could speak or react in any way, try to scale the fence maybe to help the woman, the car swerved and passed her. It halted a few feet beyond, then the door was flung open and a man leaped out.

Donna stared, mouth open, eyes wide. It was Gray!

It rocked her, seeing him there when she least expected it. And it stunned her how much she had missed him in the few hours they'd been apart.

What was he doing on the beach access road, chasing a middle-aged woman?

"Maggie, for heaven's sake, it's me!" he said as the woman halted by his car. "Who did you think was chasing you?"

"Chasing . . . ?" The woman shook her head, pushing her hair out of her eyes. "No one was chasing me, Mr. Graham. I'm doing the chasing!"

Gray sighed. "The kids?"

"Yes, the kids!" The woman wiped her damp brow with the back of one wrist. "Drat their little . . . hides!"

"Here, sit down and catch your breath." He swung open the back door and the woman flopped onto the edge of the seat, her feet resting on the ground. "What are they up to now?" he asked, and Donna saw his irrepressible grin and his dimple flash. She gripped a handful of the concealing bracken. Oh, Lord, he was good to look at!

Maggie snorted as she glared up at him. "They swiped a bowl of my special dip and two boxes of crackers! I caught them in the act, but they only laughed and ran away. I don't know why I bother to chase them, except they make me see red.

"And I don't know where they could have got to with it, either!" Now, she sounded more worried than aggrieved. "How could they disappear like that, unless they've found a way into the campground? One second they were in sight, ahead of me on the road, the next they were gone."

"Could they be along the beach in front of the campground?"

"No. They didn't make it anywhere near the beach. It was right about here they sort of . . . winked out of sight. I'll bet they've gone over that fence!" She glowered at him. "It's that Trish of yours, Mr. Graham. 'Adventuresome' is too weak a word! She wouldn't care if the worst rabble in the world slept in tents and trailers. In fact, she'd be inclined to go and check them out just for the excitement of it. Ever since her grandfather told her about the shotgun, she's been sneaking over this way the moment you bring her here, daring fate! And she doesn't care if she's leading her cousin astray! Oh, what will your father say? She's hardly been in my care ten minutes, and already she's in trouble."

So, Donna thought, Gray's little girl wasn't averse to bringing a cousin along on her vacation with her father. The ban, it seemed, extended only to Gray's friends.

Maggie sighed gustily. "I tell you, I won't have time to be picking buckshot out of their bottoms, so if they get caught in the campground, they'll just have to suffer!"

What? Donna wanted to jump out from behind the ferns and demand "What buckshot!" but held her position and her tongue. Gray laughed, and Donna had to smile. How she loved the sound of his laughter! It had the power to lift her to euphoria. Or was it simply seeing him again that did that?

"Maggie, darlin', don't you worry about it," he said, then added. "I'll take care of those kids." His tone held a note of threat, and Donna knew he

suspected the children weren't far away. Overhead, she heard the faint sounds of floorboards
squeaking.

"Humph!" Maggie obviously wasn't convinced
that Gray could take responsibility for the children. "Your father holds me accountable. I'm
getting too old for these kinds of shenanigans."

"I know, Maggie," he said, "and I promise you,
my father won't hold you accountable for this
incident. Look you take my car and drive back to
the house. I'll find those two and deal with them.
If I don't find them, I assure you they'll come
trailing home when they get good and hungry."

"With two boxes of crackers and a bowl of dip?"

"Then . . . before dark. Go now, Maggie. I know
you have plenty to do."

"Well, if you're sure . . ."

As Maggie drove away, Gray put back his head,
planted his hands on his hips, and bellowed,
"Trish! I can see where you went under the fence.
This isn't funny anymore! Both of you get back
here right now, or buckshot in your backsides will
be the least of your worries! I'm going to count
to ten, then I want your heads popping up
from wherever you've got them hidden. One . . .
two . . . three . . ."

Donna heard faint whispers overhead, then one
sharp "No" that coincided with "five." It was followed by total silence in the treehouse and a look
of growing annoyance in Gray's eyes. Or was it
worry? How must a parent feel when his child
went missing, even if he was fairly certain she was
only hiding and was really quite safe? Bad things
did happen, though, even in nice places like Cordoba Island. Donna knew that many of the land-
owners surrounding the campground looked on
campers as unsavory itinerants, the way people in

the Middle Ages had viewed Gypsies. Maybe behind Gray's piercing eyes panic was beginning to slither through his mind.

Still, did she want to tell on the children and get them in trouble? Really, was it any of her business? They were quite safe, and she knew it.

The problem was, *he* didn't.

On "nine," Donna parted the bracken and stepped out. "Hello," she said. "Fancy meeting you here."

The expression on his face made it all worthwhile.

He never did reach ten. His mouth dropped open, then closed with an audible click of his teeth as a joyous smile lit his face. He closed his eyes for a moment, then opened them again and stared at her as she took two steps closer to the fence.

"Hi," Gray said finally, very softly, when he thought there was a chance he'd be in command of his voice. Dear God, he had missed this woman. And it had been what, six, eight hours since he'd kissed her good-bye? He ached to hold her. His body burned with the need to press her against him. His hands itched to stroke over the tangled wisps of chestnut hair that had escaped her ponytail and fluttered around her face. She looked all of eighteen, and he was amazed to see that freckles were appearing on the bridge of her nose and across her cheekbones. He noted the grass clipping clinging to her bare legs and arms, the sheen of moisture on her shoulders and upper chest, the huge mower behind her, and realized what she had been doing. Hell and damnation! He should have found time to mow that big field himself. She'd mentioned that it had to be done this week. But had he thought of that? Oh, no. He'd been too intent on getting her away somewhere, away from the demanding campers and the kids who worked for her, because he'd wanted to . . .

He looked at her face again and sighed. He still wanted to. Oh, Lord, he had to touch her or go mad! What in the hell was he supposed to do about that high fence that separated them when he desperately wanted to touch her and make sure she was real? He glanced at the indentation at the foot of the wire and pictured himself sliding through on his belly as he was sure the kids had done and—

Oh, yeah. The kids.

"I . . . uh, I don't suppose you've seen a couple of stray children around in your . . . jungle over there, have you?"

Donna shook her head and said very solemnly. "No, I haven't seen anybody." As she spoke, she pointed up at the treehouse she knew he couldn't see for the foliage. All she could see was one wall, in surprisingly good condition.

Gray frowned at her, wondering what she was doing, making that strange gesture. The humor dancing in her eyes finally penetrated his thick skull and told him as much as her pointing did the whereabouts of the kids.

"Why?" she asked innocently, grinning as understanding dawned on his face. "Have you lost some children?"

He smiled, too, and the warmth of it heated her insides deliciously.

"Not really 'lost,'" he said in that voice that wrapped around her as she longed for his arms to do. "They just seem to have temporarily disappeared." He stepped forward and leaned his forearms on the fence, hooking his fingers through the links. "But," he added softly, "I find that locating them has lost much of its urgency."

Donna ignored that outwardly while inside she fluttered and twinkled and fell apart like a simpering virgin.

"And you think they might have disappeared somewhere around here?" she managed to ask with surprising calm.

He glanced at the tree she had pointed at and shrugged. "Maybe. I suppose they could be anywhere, really. I hope they haven't gone over to that side of the fence, though, because there is a distinct possibility that they'll end up with buckshot in their backsides. At least, that's the rumor we've heard."

Donna injected horror into her voice. "You mean there's somebody over here who shoots children? But that's awful!"

His straight, thick brows quirked upward for a second and he smiled again. "Not at all. Buckshot is the least of what they deserve if they're trespassing. What worries me is that if they get caught trespassing, the owner of the campground could sue us for everything we have. If that happens, then of course we wouldn't be able to afford weekly allowances, or pony feed, or pool maintenance, or any other luxury."

"Hmm, yes. I can see that would be a real problem."

"But not my problem," he said, as if suddenly dismissing the whole issue. "This may turn out to be a blessing in disguise."

She stared at his strong brown fingers curving around the galvanized wire of the fence. She couldn't help thinking of those fingers skimming over her body, the feel of them against her skin. His mouth . . .

"What—what do you mean?" she asked, forcing herself back into the act they were putting on for the listening children.

He shrugged. "Kids are costly little beasts to raise. And if those two have gone where I think they have, they might not be back. Think of the savings! So I don't think there's any point in looking further for them," he added with supreme negligence. He leaned even closer to the fence, all but pressing his face against it. "I think they're simply . . . gone."

She looked at him askance. Now what was he up to? "Gone?" she asked solemnly.

"Mm-hmm. I began to suspect it when Maggie told me how swiftly they disappeared, without a trace. I think they've been snatched into another dimension. We may never see them again, if that's the case."

She shared a smile with him and said, "How sad!" She lowered her tone sepulchrally. "I understand that happens often, especially to children. Will you miss them?"

There was a definite shrug in his tone. "For a while, I suppose. Couple of weeks, maybe. But not to worry. There's plenty more where they came from."

"Daddy!" an indignant voice called from overhead.

Donna peeked up to see a small tow-headed girl with her head and shoulders sticking out of the window opening in the treehouse. Her hair hung down around a pointed face, and she pushed twigs and leaves aside with skinny arms in a futile attempt to see her father, whom she resembled not one bit. Donna looked right through her.

"You'd miss me for more than a couple of weeks!" Trish said. "And there are no more where I came from. You can't have more kids because you aren't even married!" she added triumphantly.

As if he hadn't heard a word, Gray went on speaking to Donna, who turned her gaze back toward him. "Listen," he said, "how about dinner tonight? Good food"—he grinned and tapped himself on the chest—"and great company. And no kids to bother us."

"Daddy! I'm up here! And you never date when I'm with you!"

"Well, I suppose I could," Donna said, smiling as the leaves rustled louder and branches rattled. "I'm not busy tonight. What time?"

"Dad-*dee!*"

"I'll pick you up at eight o'clock in front of the campground office," he said pleasantly, over and through the angry sound of his daughter's voice.

"Cut it out, Daddy. You don't believe that dimension stuff any more than I do."

"Eight o'clock is fine," Donna said. "Casual or formal?" Not that it mattered. She had no intention of going, and knew that unless Gray explained things to his daughter and Trish accepted the idea of his dating—which didn't sound likely—the date would remain nothing more than an idea with which to torment Trish.

"Daddy!"

"Oh, casual," Gray said with a pointed look at her bare shoulder where her tank-top strap had slid down. His smile was decidedly lascivious. "Let's say it's come-as-you-are. We'll be barbecuing. At my dad's place. And bring a bathing suit."

"Thanks," she said, trying with all her might to keep her hand off her tank-top strap. She didn't want him to know how the hot lick of his gaze was almost palpable on her skin. It was a hard battle, but she won it. "I'd love to come. But there's no need to pick me up. I can get myself there."

He smiled. "Well, if you're—" He leaped back as a small pink running shoe sailed out of the tree, clattering through leaves and branches, and smacked into the fence not an inch from his nose.

"Daddy! You're making me mad! Who is that lady?"

"What's this?" he said, stepping back from the fence. He looked up toward the thick leaves, though Donna knew he and his daughter were invisible to each other. "A message from the tenth dimension?"

"Don't be silly," the little girl said scathingly. "You know you could hear me all along. You only pretended not to, to tease us."

"Just as you were only hiding in that tree to tease me. And Maggie. Maggie deserves better than that, you know. I'm going to expect the pair of you to apologize to her . . . and mean it. And to make sure that you do mean it, you're both barred from the pool for the rest of the weekend."

There was a furious wail from inside the tree-house, the sounds of a struggle, then the blond head was replaced by one capped with short dark hair. A pair of intensely angry eyes bored down, searching for the man. Not finding him, they fixed themselves on Donna. "You can't do that, Uncle Graham! I have to *prac*tice!"

"Too bad," Gray said with a total lack of sympathy. "You should have thought of that earlier. You've been warned about trespassing over there." When this was met with a stream of hair-curling curses, Gray added sternly, "And you've been warned about that kind of language too. No pool for a week."

"You aren't the boss of me! I can do what I want!"

"Then what you 'want' better be coming down out of that tree and getting back on this side of the fence where you belong," Gray said grimly. "Both of you. And fast."

The dark head disappeared. There were more thuds, then the squeak of the rusty hinges again, and a thump as the hatch closed. Shortly, two small, grubby children of approximately the same age pushed their way out of the hollow tree trunk and stopped, staring warily at her.

She stared back. Gray's daughter wore torn neon pink and green shorts and a bright blue blouse with two buttons missing. For a moment she felt dizzy. Trish was nine. Was this what her own daughter would have been like, had she lived, had Jamie and Donna married and raised her together on Cordoba Island the way they had dreamed? Would she have the same tough, reedy look about her, the same healthy, outdoor glow? For a moment Donna wanted to gather the child close and hold her, pretend a little. A little Kincaid girl, all her own.

The boy, whom she'd all but ignored while her gaze ate up Gray's daughter, was wearing only skimpy black Lycra swim trunks. He was slightly shorter than his cousin, probably a year or so younger, with tightly curled dark hair that shone reddish in the sun, and peeling sunburn on freckled shoulders and nose. Fists clenched, he took one step closer to her, looking so fiercely protective that Donna smiled at his instinctive masculine aggression.

She held her hands out at her sides, palms up. "Look. No shotgun. And I want to assure you that you're welcome to use my treehouse anytime you want, as long as your family agrees."

"Your treehouse?" The little boy stared, his brown eyes wide and round.

"Yes," she said. "My uncle owns this campground. I helped build that treehouse and—"

She broke off as he gasped. "Tyler French is your uncle?"

"That's right," she said, and both children stared at her in horror. Trish clapped a hand over her mouth and the boy shoved his jaw out belligerently, even as he backed away. Then, before she could speak again, they turned and bolted, slithering on their bellies under the fence, Trish stopping halfway through and scrambling back to get her shoe. When she emerged on the other side, she was missing yet another button and both children bore new streaks of grime. They cast another horrified look at her, evaded Gray, and took off up the road, their feet making splatting sounds in the soft dust. Donna wondered how they would have reacted if she'd said she was Dracula's daughter.

Gray looked at her, smiling wryly as he read the expression on her face. Half apologetically, he said, "The campground has a bit of a reputation as a dangerous place, you know, so as the niece of its owner, you must be treated with extreme caution."

She looked at him, disbelieving, and laughed outright. "The shotgun I heard you and Maggie talking about? The buckshot?"

"You got it."

"Good Lord! I thought the two of you were joking, trying to impress the kids! But why would they believe that if they don't believe the tenth dimension?"

"Well, largely because they've been hearing the buckshot story for a lot longer than the other stuff. I simply made that up as I went along." He grinned. "With your help. You're a good ad-libber, my lovely Ms. Mailer."

She was too incensed to listen to compliments. "You made it up exactly as somebody made up the story of this place being protected by a shotgun," she said indignantly, then frowned. "Unless . . . Ah, no! That louse! Oh, Gray, how could he do that? As if everything else weren't bad enough, character assassination on top of it is simply too much. I'm glad he's gone! I have a good mind to track him down and take him to court for slander."

"Who?"

"The manager." Wading through long grass, she approached the fence.

"Donna . . ." He shook his head slowly. "It wasn't the manager who made those threats. It was your uncle, a few years back. My dad told me he phoned over to our house in a towering rage and said that anybody who tried to trespass on his place was going to be met with a shower of buckshot. That was just after Jamie was killed and Dad had moved out here permanently. Dad didn't want to lose any more of his family, and he laid down strict orders that the kids were to stay away from here and told them the consequences of disobedience."

"I don't believe that for one minute!" Donna exclaimed. "Oh, I believe your father probably told the kids that, but Uncle Tyler has never owned a gun in his life. He despises them. And as for him shooting at a child, the idea's ludicrous!"

She shook the fence. "This is to keep the campers from straying and trespassing on neighbors' properties, you father's primarily, because he made so much trouble. Uncle Ty had to install it at great cost, all the way around, even up and through the woods! He had to renew his mortgage to do it. Dammit, Gray, I remember that! I was here when it happened!" That she was also the one who'd swiped the wire cutters and helped Jamie snip his way through after that, she didn't say.

"All right, all right, calm down." He stroked her fingers, which she'd curled through the links of the fence.

She snatched her hands away. "I'm not going to calm down! I want you to go home and tell those kids that I meant what I said. They're welcome to come over and play in treehouse anytime they want and there won't be any trouble from me. By heaven, I'll even put a gate in for them!" Obviously, Jamie's "gate" had long since been repaired, since the kids were sliding underneath. "However, if your father wants them to stay out, he's going to have to tell them it's for his own reasons—such as his snobbery—and not because they have to fear anybody over here. I hope I've made that clear!"

"Hey, come on! It wasn't me who told the kids that story."

She glared at him. "But you carried it on."

Gray closed his eyes and leaned his forehead against the fence. He'd let the story go on because he'd believed it, but how could he tell her that? He should have checked it out for himself. Why hadn't he? Hell, he knew his father, knew how he loved to manipulate. Knew he was more than capable of having come up with a story like that simply to keep Jimmy from associating with campground kids.

He lifted his head and looked at her, yearning to reach through the fence, to reach her. "Donna . . . sweetheart," he said with sudden urgency, "I wasn't kidding about your coming over to the house tonight. So come, come and give my father that message yourself. I'd love to see his face when you do it." His eyes softened. "I want to touch you, hold you, kiss you. Oh, God, I want to make love to you again." He groaned. "Can I come over now?"

She wanted so much to say yes, to magically part the links of the fence that separated them and melt into his embrace. "No, Gray. I can't. We can't. There's your daughter, for one thing."

His face tightened, his eyes looked tortured. "I'll tell her. I promise I will. Hell, she's not stupid. She's known all along that I might fall in love someday."

"Then tell her, Gray. But until you do, until she knows and understands that I'm no threat to her, I'd rather not risk hurting her."

"I don't know if I can do that the first day of our vacation together," he said miserably. "Ah, sweetheart, please come for dinner tonight. I need to be with you."

As soon as he said it, he regretted the words. She looked so forlorn, biting that full lower lip that he ached so badly to kiss. Before he could recant his request, she said slowly, "It's more than just your daughter, Gray. There is also the simple, inescapable fact that your father wouldn't want me in his home."

"He's going to have to get over that, then, isn't he?" Gray asked gently, letting her know that she was more important to him than his father's approval.

"That," she said, stepping back from the fence,

"is something you're going to have to take up with him, Gray."

"All right, I will. And believe me, if I don't get you an engraved invitation, personally signed by my father, I'll chew my way through this fence before the night's out."

"If you did that," she said, trying to laugh, "your father would probably sue me for not keeping my guests and their pets adequately contained."

"Hey, are you scared of my father?"

She hesitated. "I don't know. I guess I was, once."

"Don't be. Not ever again. I won't let him hurt you."

At his words, her mouth trembled, and it struck him that maybe Jamie hadn't waited until he was twenty to take even the slightest interest in the opposite sex. Maybe there had been more than a simple little childhood friendship between Donna and his brother. Jamie had certainly been immature enough to be taken in by that older woman who had given him such a hell of a time. Perhaps that immaturity had appealed to the sixteen-year-old Donna. Could it be that *Jamie* had been the "difference of opinion" she'd had with her aunt and uncle? Gray thought about it for a minute, then dismissed it. Almost.

He dropped his hands from the fence and stepped back, his gaze still holding hers. "In case it hasn't occurred to you, I'm not a terrified teenager my father can intimidate. Remember that, Donna. I'm an adult. A very determined adult. I choose my own friends. And I make my own rules." He smiled. "Tonight, love."

"No." With a last look at him, she strode back to the mower. She remounted it and brought it to noisy life, then cut a broad swath as she roared toward the far side of the meadow. When she reached the end of the cut and turned, Gray was not in sight.

She told herself that her eyes were tearing because of the thick pollen in the air.

Eight

It wasn't an engraved invitation, but it was, to Donna's surprise, a handwritten one. And hand delivered. It arrived within a couple of hours of her having left Gray at the fence.

She crumpled it and tossed it in the garbage can by the back door.

"Sure," she said. "Sure, Chester Kincaid, I'll just bet you're as 'sincere' as you sign yourself. I'll just bet you wish to have me join you and your guests for a barbecue this evening. And I'll just bet you have an offer to make me that you're certain I can't refuse."

But still, the opportunity to see Gray again was tempting. She retrieved the invitation and smoothed it out, wondering if Gray was behind her having received it. Dammit, she would go. She loved Gray and he said he loved her. Maybe it was time she faced down Chester Kincaid once and for all.

Andy, who had agreed to stay on duty and would even spend the night in case she was out very late, whistled at her as she came out of her bedroom in a short powder-blue jumpsuit with full, flirty legs and a halter top. She'd cinched it at the waist with a wide white leather belt, and wore white wedge-heeled thong sandals. "Awesome!" he said.

Donna took that as approval, and left for the Kincaid home in a much easier state of mind.

Maggie, looking only slightly less frazzled than earlier in the day, answered the door to Donna's ring. She ushered her through the house and out the back to where the guests were assembled in moving clusters as bright as the huge umbrellas that blosssomed all over the place. Standing at the edge of a cedar deck, Donna scanned the throng for a familiar face. She was hoping for one and deeply dreading the other.

She saw Gray two levels down, part of a laughing group lounging around a table laden with drinks and trays of hors d'oeuvres. Though he'd given no appearance of a man awaiting the arrival of a certain guest, as she moved toward the broad, shallow steps leading down to the level where he sat, he leaped to his feet and swept his gaze over her.

"You're here!" She saw him mouth the words as he gave the woman he'd been sitting beside an absent pat on the arm. Then he came striding toward her, his smile turning her inside out. The sight of him nearly undid her. Her hands shook so hard, it scared her. She linked them tightly together.

"Hi," he said. He took her hands in his and spread them apart as he ran his gaze over her. She knew her jumpsuit made her legs look longer and more slender than they actually were, and showed off her evenly tanned arms and shoulders. Still, the appreciation in his eyes was a welcome boost to her self-confidence.

"You look beautiful!" If he noticed the tremor in her fingers, he didn't comment. "But you certainly didn't come as you were." he slid a hand up her arm and curled it over her shoulder—the one the tank-top strap had slid off. "I think I like this even better. I'm really glad you came, Donna, and I wish there weren't so damned many people around, because I want to kiss you properly."

"Your father invited me," she said.

"Ah, but I did it first." Quickly he bent and took her lips in a short but very telling kiss, then stood back, still looking at her in appreciation. She took the opportunity to return his stare.

His oatmeal-colored shorts, several shades paler than his bronzed legs, were obviously from some European designer's summer collection, as was his fashionably wrinkled pale yellow cotton shirt, open partway down his chest and with the sleeves rolled nearly to his shoulders. He looked wonderful, and she longed to pretend she was there to enjoy his company, enjoy the party, but she knew it wasn't true. There was business to conduct, and the sooner she got it over with, the sooner she could move on to . . . other things.

"Am I likely to meet Trish tonight?" she asked, and thought he looked uncomfortable. All right, so he hadn't told his daughter yet. She shouldn't be disappointed. It was still only the first day of their vacation.

"The kids are sleeping aboard my dad's boat tonight," he said.

"I see. Then I suppose I should go and say hello to your father. He says he has an offer I won't be able to refuse."

"That might be true."

Gray looked away from her, still unnerved by his father's extremely violent response to the news, blurted out by Trish, that Tyler French's niece was back at Clearwater Camping. He'd never forget the terrible rage Chester had succumbed to, the irrational demands that Gray "get that damned woman off this island! Now! Today!"

For a couple of incredible moments he'd been seriously afraid of his father, then afraid *for* him. Finally, he'd simply been appalled.

Turning back to Donna, he said urgently, "Do me a favor, will you? Take my father's offer. It is a good one. A very good one. Take it, please, and get off this island."

"What? Why?"

"Because . . . it would be safer."

"For whom?" For him, she wondered, because he couldn't keep his hands off her and didn't want to upset his family?

He jammed a hand through his hair. "I'm not sure. I don't know. Maybe I'm going crazy." He laughed roughly as he caught her by the wrists, holding her before him. "Maybe it's just a symptom of falling in love, but I'm afraid for you. My father's acting strangely, and I don't want you hurt."

Hurt? His father couldn't possibly hurt her more than he already had. She wanted to tell Gray that she wasn't afraid of Chester anymore. He'd done his worst to her, and she'd survived.

"Strangely?" she asked. "How?"

Gray stared into her face, wanting to tell her, but how could he? He didn't understand it himself, and "strangely" really didn't cover it.

For ten minutes Chester had bellowed and sworn and thrown furniture around his den, leaving Gray no longer doubting his mother's quietly stated reason for having left her first husband: She couldn't raise her child with a man whose temper made him unpredictable if crossed.

His hold gentled on Donna's wrists, and he slid his hands up to her elbows, then wrapped them around her waist. One thing he didn't want was her frightened—especially of him. "All I'm saying, love, is if my father's offer is what you want, even close to what you want, don't hold out for anything more. Take the money and go." He smiled, tightening his hands around her and pulling her close enough for her to feel the heat emanating from his body. "And wait for me in Victoria. Because you and I, one way or another, are going to be together, Donna. Remember that. Just get away from the campground."

She slipped free of him and walked the few steps back up to the main deck. Pausing, she turned and looked down at him. "I'll make that decision when I've listened to your father's offer, and not before."

He drew in a deep breath and nodded. "Fine, then. Why don't we see if he's ready now?"

The three of them met on the second-floor balcony, Chester watching her and Gray ascend the stairs toward him. How had he known to be there at precisely that time? Donna wondered. Or had he been there all along, watching over them like a vulture, waiting for the right moment to swoop?

Meeting Chester Kincaid for the first time in ten years was far harder than she'd feared it would be. Her knees weakened and her throat tightened. For a bad moment she felt sixteen again, sixteen and frightened, shamed, embarrassed—because now other people knew what she and Jamie had been doing together for most of the summer. Because now, what had been such a beautiful expression of their brand-new love seemed dirty and wrong and disgraceful, once bared to the scrutiny of other eyes.

Forcing herself to be pleasant even if it killed her—in spite of everything else, this man was Gray's father—she extended her hand.

"Good evening, Chester," she said, and watched with satisfaction as his eyes narrowed and his nostrils flared. He had not been expecting her to say "Chester" with confidence, but "Mr. Kincaid" with cowering diffidence and subservience.

He recovered swiftly. "Hello, my dear," he said in a kindly, avuncular tone, taking her hand and holding it warmly between his own. "It came as a great surprise when Graham told me you were in charge of the campground. I had no idea you were back on this coast."

"I came a couple of weeks ago," she said, meeting his gaze unfalteringly. "And a good thing, too, because the manager walked out on the job for no apparent reason. I was glad to be here to relieve Uncle Tyler of the worries about the place."

"I'm sure you were," he said. His jovial laugh sounded, to Donna, forced. She pulled her hand free, unable to bear his touch another second.

"Come along inside," he went on, turning her toward a pair of black sliding-glass doors. "We'll get down to business right away, shall we, so we can enjoy the party. But may I order you a drink?"

"No, thank you," she said, managing to twist her elbow free of his clasp. How could the man be so affable? How could he act as if they were old friends? How was she going to keep from throwing up if he didn't turn off this disgusting, oily charm?

As the three of them took seats, Chester behind his desk, Donna directly in front of him, Gray off to one side, Chester's smile faded. His hooded eyes under thick white brows took on an almost predatory look, and he quietly made Donna an offer the likes of which she hadn't anticipated in her wildest dreams.

"I . . ." For a second she was without words, without breath. She blinked and shook her head, while Chester watched her in amusement.

"What's the trouble, my dear? Have I surprised you so very much?"

"Yes." She managed to draw in enough air to supply her brain with a minimum of oxygen. "Yes, you have. That's a very generous offer."

She didn't say, "What's the catch?" but she wanted to.

"I'm a generous man," he said, leaning back in his swivel chair and folding his hands over his belly. "I've had my lawyer drawing up the necessary papers since I knew you had returned to the island. He flew the contract in today."

Well! Chester Kincaid moved fast when he moved, obviously a characteristic he had in common with his elder son.

If Chester hadn't been willing to pay Sadie and Tyler a fair price, what had changed, she wondered, now that she was on the scene? She glanced at Gray as another thought whipped across her whirling mind, and she nearly laughed aloud. No! Surely Chester didn't want her gone because he was afraid that yet another one of his sons would succumb to her "wiles."

It couldn't be that, but whatever he was up to, she was on guard. She knew she couldn't trust him one short inch. Narrowing her eyes, she accepted the sheaf of papers he slid toward her. She sat back in her chair to read the document, and was surprised to see Gray pick up an identical sheaf and scan it himself.

"Come now, come now," Chester said chidingly when she turned the first page and began the second. "Surely you don't have to read every word, my dear. Let's not fool ourselves. We laypeople never fully understand legal documents anyway. Here, use my pen."

She glanced up. "Thank you." She took the pen and set it on the desk, then she read every word of every page, slowly, carefully, thoughtfully, aware of Chester's growing impatience. He shifted in his chair, got up and paced to the window, then turned and strode back and flung himself down again, making overburdened springs squeak alarmingly. She refused to be disturbed by it.

When she was finished, she stacked the pages neatly again by tapping them on the desk. "Apart from one or two clauses I can't agree to, it seems perfectly straightforward. I'll have my attorney look it over and get back to you as soon as possible."

"What?" Chester snapped erect. His eyes were sharp, his brows drawn together. "What the hell are you talking about? That's a perfectly good agreement, and there's nothing to stop you signing it right this minute!" He stood abruptly and thrust the fountain pen into her face. "Sign."

"Not before I have the agreement okayed by my own lawyer," Donna said firmly, folding the papers once.

"Dammit, didn't Graham make it clear—" With a look of censure that should have withered his son, Chester broke off, breathing hard. "This is a one-time offer, miss. Take it or leave it." Spittle formed in one corner of his mouth. "Tonight!"

"Dad, take it easy. Donna's completely right to want her own lawyer to see the agreement before she signs."

"You keep out of this!" Chester shouted. "If her lawyer has to okay this, that means the deal doesn't go through until Tuesday at the earliest!"

"So what?" Gray said. "What difference will another two or three days make?"

Chester glared at Donna, then at his son. "I wanted the deal closed today. I made that clear! You were supposed to take care of it, Graham!"

Donna shot to her feet and stared at Gray, feeling ill. Was that what he'd been doing all week, as well as last night? "Taking care" of it?

Chester smiled slyly at Donna. "I merely thought You'd be anxious, my dear, to be done with the place."

She fixed him with a hard stare. "Not so eager that I'm willing to agree to terms that force me to move off the island within twenty-four hours of signing. I also want a provision calling for all prior bookings to be honored until the end of the current season."

Chester threw his shoulders back. "Absolutely not!"

"Then I'm afraid I'll have to decline your offer," she said quietly, keeping her face blank. "I have an obligation to the people who booked their vacations with us. They have every right to expect those reservations to be honored. We have guests planning to come right up to the end of September."

"Cancel them."

"I can't do that. If you want me to sign this agreement, then I want that clause added. Without it, I might have to consider taking the business off the market until the season is over."

She smiled at the expression of disbelief on Chester's face.

"By then," she went on, "the market may have

picked up and I'll be getting offers like this every week. Or, I might simply decide to stay." That, she recognized, was her biggest ace in the hole. Chester Kincaid hated Donna Mailer even more than he hated the campground. And he wanted her off Cordoba Island, as much as, if more than, he wanted the business closed down.

Chester leaned toward her, his posture intimidating. "The market's not going to pick up soon enough for anybody else to make you the kind of offer I've made. I'm buying that property, miss, one way or another, and I have no intention of becoming a campground operator."

"Donna has a valid point," Gray said, earning himself an indignant snort from his father. "As she said, those bookings were made in good faith. Common sense, common humanity, forces us to honor them until the end of this season if we take over the campground."

Chester scowled at his son. His mouth was taut, his jaw squared. "You mean *when* we take possession of that property! Dammit, Graham, I didn't make you vice president in charge of acquisitions just so you could act like a bloody bleeding heart every time somebody gives you a tale of woe. I told you I wanted that girl off—"

Chester broke off and turned back to Donna. "I suggest you give my offer—as it stands—serious consideration, young woman. You have until midnight tonight to think it over. After that, every day's delay means a five-thousand-dollar drop in my offer."

Donna stared him down, thinking on her feet. What would Uncle Tyler do if he were there? Would he sell the place, regardless of what subsequently happened to it, if the price was right?

She lifted her chin. Uncle Tyler had not wanted

to make that decision. That was why he had given it to her to handle. Picking up the papers, she folded them yet another time. "As I said, I'll be in touch as soon as my lawyer has had a chance to look over this agreement. Good evening, gentlemen." Turning on her heel, she marched to the door, slid it open, and stepped out into a brisk wind that had blown up as darkness fell.

Gray caught her halfway down the stairs. "Where are you off to so fast?"

"Home," she said, twisting her elbow free.

"You were invited for dinner," he reminded her. "The barbecue is about to be served. The fireworks—"

"No, thank you." At the bottom of the stairs, she turned to face him. "You did your part, Gray."

"Dammit, that's not—"

"Isn't it?" she challenged him, eyes angry, face flushed. "I'm sorry if you're in trouble because I didn't act exactly as predicted and sign on the dotted line like a good little girl, properly mesmerized by the vice president in charge of acquisitions." She rushed on when he would have interrupted. "But I'm sure your father will forgive you if you grovel properly. After all, even you can't be expected to acquire everything you're sent after.

"Good night, and thank you for your . . . hospitality."

"Donna, wait!" He lunged after here, but she slipped away around the corner of the house. Following, he ran into a flying umbrella. Caught by the wind, it had tipped over the table it had been anchored in and was tumbling across the deck, trailing shattering bottles and glasses and chased by a startled bartender.

By the time Gray had untangled himself and reached the front of the house, Donna was in her car and driving away. He watched her taillights wink out of sight and considered pursuit. But no. Better, he thought, to let her cool down. He'd have his talk with Trish in the morning, then go to Donna with everything open before them, free and clear to explore every facet of their love.

Because Donna Mailer, not her uncle's campground, was one acquisition he meant to make. Not for his father. Oh, no. That one would be all for himself.

Nine

Unable to rest, Donna wandered along the shore-line. Why had she run out on Gray without giving him a chance? she asked herself. She loved him, didn't she? Why was it so hard to trust him? Maybe she should go back, talk to him. But what could she say? How could she explain her almost instinctive distrust?

She sat on a large, dry log and gazed at the bright lights dotting the Kincaid's many decks, listened to the music flying in fits and starts toward her in the rising, gusty wind, and knew she wouldn't go back, not with all those people there. What she had to discuss with Gray needed privacy, security.

As she watched she saw the Kincaid cruiser pitching and tossing in the center of the bay, beyond the shelter of the breakwater. She hoped the wind and swell would die down by morning. Most of her guests had small boats, and they'd be harbor-bound if the weather was bad. She sighed. Another black mark against Clearwater Camping.

The dark waves curled in, their creamy tops frothing up onto the sand, sending spirals of phosphorescence outward. Donna listened to them rushing in . . . receding . . . pausing . . . repeating. It was a sound she normally found soothing, but tonight she didn't. She felt restless, troubled, in need of something.

No. Someone. Gray.

Kicking off her shoes, she wandered out into the water until she was ankle-deep, with waves washing up to her knees. She tilted her head back and looked up, wishing for the moon—a tiny fingernail of light descending toward the horizon—wishing for the stars—as far out of reach as the peace and happiness she longed for. All she knew was a growing ache of loneliness deep within.

The susurration of the water whispered his name, and her heart echoed it. *Gray . . . Gray . . . Gray . . .* Though she tried to still it, it continued to whisper along with the waves. *Gray, Gray, Gray . . .*

"Ouch! Dammit! Cruddy rocks! Ugh! Seaweed! Get the hell off me! Gaaah!"

Donna whirled in response to the tremulous voice and violent splashing, recognizing at once who had swum ashore on her beach. She nearly fell, but caught herself and stared at the small wet figure emerging from the ocean a few yards away, shaking water from his hair and wiping it from his eyes. He reeled and tried to wade back out. Banging into the rocks at the end of the arc of sand, he let loose another stream of curses. As Donna lunged toward him he was caught by a wave and bashed to his knees. He came up cussing again, using words she'd seldom heard. A dark streak, blood, she was sure, ran down his leg.

"Hold on," she shouted, splashing through the shallows toward him. "I'm coming. I'll help you!"

He'd come in at the only part of the beach where weed- and barnacle-covered rocks made the footing treacherous and swimming unwise. "What in the world are you doing here at this time of night?" She reached for the child, steadied him, and tried to lift him over the worst of the rocks. He struggled against her hold, flinching back and falling again.

"No!" he screamed. "You leave me alone! Don't you touch me! I'll tell my grandpa if you hurt me! Get away! Get away!" He tried to fight her off, but lost his balance again, falling against her. He shook with cold, and probably exhaustion. He was, after all, only a little boy. Over his protests, she picked him up. His struggles soon became feeble, though his mouth remained as foul as any she'd ever heard. His skin was cold, and he shivered violently as she rushed up the path toward the house with him in her arms, his wet body soaking her clothes with cold seawater, his tears hot on her shoulder.

Though he could cuss like a pirate, when overwhelmed by a superior force, he cried like any other child, with the weary resignation of the powerless. "I'm sorry, lady. I'm sorry. I'll leave. I'll go away. I didn't mean to come to the campground. Just to the treehouse. Let me go, please let me go, lady. Please don't tell the man with the gun . . ."

"Hush, now. Hush," she said soothingly. "I'm not going to hurt you, honey. And there is no man with a gun. Remember? We met earlier today and I said you could use the treehouse whenever you want, so there's nothing to be afraid of."

"But he's your uncle. You'll have to tell him."

"Sure he's my uncle, but he won't hurt you, and neither will I. Besides," she added, "my uncle isn't here."

That seemed to calm him. He was quieter as she mounted the steps to the front porch, though he still cried in hard, choking spurts.

"What were you doing swimming at this time of night?" she asked. "You could have been swept away by the tide, and no one would have seen you." Or heard, with all the music at the Kincaids'. Then, remembering what Gray had said about Trish sleeping aboard the boat, she gasped. "Oh, no! You were on the boat, weren't you? What happened? Did you fall overboard?"

"No," he said, struggling to get down as she propped him on one knee and wrenched open the door. "I jumped overboard."

"What?" She carried him inside. "Why? You could have drowned!"

"Not me. I'm a good swimmer. I'm on the swim team at school."

She thought he looked hardly old enough to go to school, let alone be on a swim team.

The warmer air of the house seemed to revive him. "Let me go, dammit!" he demanded, managing to land a punch on her throat.

"I'm not letting you go anywhere," she said hoarsely, her larynx aching from his blow. This was one mean, mad little kid she'd rescued, though he might not agree with her assessment of what she'd done. More likely, he'd call it a capture.

Tightening her grip on him, making sure both his hands were pinned, she continued. "What I'm doing is getting you warmed up before you go into shock from hypothermia, then I'm going to phone your grandfather's house and let them know where you are. They'll be frantic if they know you're missing."

He continued to struggle all the way across the kitchen, but when she rolled him in a blanket on the couch, he subsided, the warmth no doubt hitting him like a sledgehammer. He hugged his arms tightly around himself and cried, his face buried in a cushion.

"I don't want to go home! I won't go home. You can't send me back! Please, lady!"

"Come on, honey," she said, "let me get you dried off a bit and see to your cut knee. You have to get warmed up, you know, or you'll get very, very sick." She looked at his blue lips, his pinched nostrils, his shriveled fingertips and trembling limbs. Lord! Even his shrunken looking belly quivered.

He didn't answer, only huddled in the blanket and wiped his face with the back of one hand while he continued to cry. Donna darted into the bathroom and came back with a first aid kit and a thick towel. She tossed the towel over his head before disinfecting his barnacle scrape and putting a bandage on it. Then, standing before him, his forehead pressed against her middle, she toweled his hair briskly until it no longer dripped down his face and shoulders, but stood in stiff little peaks and curls, sticky with salt.

He glared at her resentfully, but was shivering too hard to try to escape. He was so cute in his mute defiance that she wanted to take him on her lap and hug him and baby him and love him half to death, but she didn't dare. He was all elbows and knees, jutting lower lip, squared chin, and impotent fury, not a kid who'd take kindly to hugs from strangers. She thought he probably wouldn't take kindly to hugs from his own mother when he was in this frame of mind.

She tossed the towel aside and smiled at him. "You like hot chocolate?"

He nodded, looking only fractionally less rebellious. Still wary, his gaze darted around the room as if he trusted no one, not even a woman who dried his hair, warmed his shivers, and offered him hot chocolate. As if the wicked old man with the shotgun might leap out from behind a door, bellowing, "Ready, aim, fire!" at any moment.

"It's okay. Honestly," she said as she sat a cup of milk in the mircowave. "The only other person in this house is Andy, my helper, and he's asleep in there." She nodded toward the hallway. As the milk heated she continued in a calm, conversational tone, "You know, it puzzles me, why you'd jump overboard at this time of night."

"Whadda you care?"

She shrugged and met his angry brown stare. "Maybe I don't. Maybe I'm just curious. Or maybe I'm a mean old busybody who's about to call your uncle and let him ask you the questions you're going to have to answer sooner or later."

He glowered sullenly, and for an instant she thought she saw a resemblance to someone. But who? "What I do gots nothin' to do with Uncle Graham. He might be the boss of Trish, but not me. I told you, I'm going to the treehouse. I'm gonna sleep there."

He glared at her mutinously, but the effect was spoiled by the sobs that continued to catch in his chest and shake his shoulders. He poked a hand out of the blanket and wiped his nose. "You said I could go there anytime I wanted."

She couldn't help herself. His plea, for that was

what it was, affected her deeply and she sat beside him, cuddling him close. "Well, sure I did, honey, but not at eleven o'clock at night, when you're sopping wet and half-frozen."

To her amazement, after a moment's stiffness, he slumped against her, burrowing for warmth. "Besides," she added, "swimming ashore wasn't a good idea, even if it wasn't nighttime. How did you plan to get warm and dry when you got to the treehouse?"

He lifted his head from her bosom. "I don't know." He shrugged, one skinny shoulder appearing out of the cocoon of blanket. She wrapped him warmly again, keeping her arm around him. "I didn't think about that. I just had to get off the boat." His eyes flooded and he wiped them, along with his nose, on the blanket. "I c-couldn't stay out there any longer! It got windy and the water got rough and then I got sick! I *hate* throwing up!"

"Of course you do. Everyone does." The microwave beeped and she stood to stir chocolate mix into the milk. Sitting beside him again, she helped him get his hands out of the folds of blanket while remaining mostly covered, then gave him the cup. "Couldn't you just have asked to be taken ashore?"

"No. Grandpa said I had to stay there all night."

"Because of the party?"

He wrapped his hands around the hot mug. "I guess so." He fixed his misery-filled gaze on her face. "I didn't mean to get sick. I can't help it! But Grandpa calls me a big baby when I get seasick."

Donna thought Grandpa should be keelhauled and thrown to the sharks. And where in hell was his uncle when this kind of abuse was taking place? She said nothing, though, waiting in sympathetic silence for him to go on.

His eyes flooded over again, and the tears dripped into his hot chocolate. Tenderly, Donna wiped them away with her thumb. "I know he was mad at me for coming to the campground today," the boy said, "and wanted me out of his sight, but I couldn't stay on the boat that long. I hate the damn boat!" He sniffled loudly and wiped his nose on the blanket again. Donna leaned over and snapped a tissue from the nearby box. She dried his face, then held it to his nose.

He blew. "And it was all because Trish told him we'd been caught over here in this stupid campground. I don't know why she had to go and do that. She knows how mad he gets if I come here. I told her and told her my treehouse had to be a secret, but she had to go and blab!"

His eyes widened as he added in a subdued tone, as if suddenly remembering, "Boy, Grandpa was mad. It was awesome. I've never seen him that mad, and I've seen him mad lots of times. He yelled. He tossed a chair right through the window. He smashed his computer screen with the phone. His face got all funny looking and his mouth made lots of spit."

The boy's hands shook and he took a big gulp of his hot chocolate, leaving a mustache on his upper lip. He looked like such a sweet little angel that Donna could scarcely contain her shocked laughter when he said in a growl so much like his grandfather's voice, "That damn Trish! She's such a hopeless little bitch I'd like to strangle her!" She choked the laughter back as she realized how like Chester the child was in mannerisms.

She stared at the boy. If he was Gray's nephew, son of one of his siblings, why, when he brought him to Chester Kincaid's home, was he not in charge of the boy? And why did this child call Chester "Grandpa"?

"What's your name?" she asked, feeling a chill creep over her, one that had nothing to do with her soaked clothing.

He lifted his chin haughtily. "James Alexander Kincaid."

The cold became an icy deluge. "I see. And who . . ." She licked her lips, swallowed dryly. "Who is your father?"

"My father's dead. He was Jamie Kincaid. My name's the same as his, so they called me Jimmy so we'd know who they meant when they spoke to us." He shrugged. "That's what Grandpa told me and . . ."

The rest of what he said was lost within the ringing inside Donna's head.

My father's dead . . . Her head spun. Her stomach rolled. Her knees felt wobbly even though she was sitting down. *He was Jamie Kincaid.* Her throat ached. She wanted to put her head down and weep. Jamie's son. And clearly as unhappy as Jamie had been, being raised by Jamie's father. Why? What about Jimmy's mother? And why had it been all right for Jamie to have a child with someone else, when the baby that he'd given *her* had been unwanted? Why hadn't the other girl, or woman, been forced to discard her baby too? What had made the difference? Jimmy must be only a year or so younger than her daughter would have been, so it couldn't have been that Jamie had matured so very much and been capable of defying his father.

Unless . . . unless he'd loved the other girl a lot more than he'd loved her.

"Yes," she managed to say fairly evenly, becoming aware that Jimmy was watching her, looking at her strangely. "I can see how different nick-names would be necessary."

Though she spoke rationally, the aching sixteen-year-old girl in her cried, *It isn't fair! It isn't fair! It isn't fair!*

"Where is your mother?" she asked.

Jimmy snorted and thrust the blanket aside as he got to his feet. "That bitch! Who the hell knows where she is? And who cares?"

He interpreted her stare as argument.

"That's what she is!" he said. "She ran away and left me the minute I was born. Grandpa says she didn't want a baby. She was going to put me up for 'doption, let strangers have me 'cause she wanted to be a singer and a baby would have got in her way. He found out what she wanted to do and rescued me."

"Your grandfather? Not—not your father?"

He sniffled again. "He was around part of the time, but he had things to do." Jimmy tilted his chin up proudly again. "'Portant stuff."

He held the pose for only a moment, before his chin dropped and his mouth quivered. "Then . . . Grandma left, too, after my dad got killed." His face crumpled, and Donna swept him onto her lap and held him close as he cried for several minutes.

"I don't get to see my grandma much anymore 'cause Grandpa won't let me go where she lives," he said finally, his voice muffled as he let her hold him. "Grandpa says women are fickle and we don't need one around. He says we'll do okay together, that we don't need a grandmother or a mother to look after us."

He paused for a moment, then added, "But I wish my mom hadn't wanted to be a singer more than she wanted to be my mom."

Donna swallowed the ache in her throat as she

pressed his head against the one in her chest.
This could have been her child. He should have
been! Maybe, if she and Jamie had married, her
baby wouldn't have died and Jamie wouldn't have
died and . . . "And is—is your mother a singer?"

Jimmy began shivering again as he shrugged. "I
dunno," he said dully. "Prob'ly not. Grandpa says
she's more'n likely a hooker somewhere. That's
what she was destined for. Whoredom."

Donna shook her head. "You have quite a vo-
cabulary for a kid your age, you know." Privately,
she thought he spent too much time with his
grandfather, was overly influenced by him and his
attitudes, especially his attitudes toward women.

"Grandpa says she was nothing but a little slut
who wanted to get her hands on his money and
tried to do it by getting pregnant so my dad would
have to marry her."

Poor Chester! Two in a row. "And did he? Marry
your mother?" she asked.

"Nah. He was only twenty. Guys are too young
to get married at that age, Grandpa says. He says
a man shouldn't get married until he'd old enough
to handle a woman, teach her to behave properly.
He had two wives, and they didn't behave right, so
he had to get rid of them. I don't think I'm gonna
get married until I'm old. Maybe thirty." Lifting his
head, he looked up at her. "Are you married?"

The roaring in her ears nearly blocked his last
question, but she managed to hold on to her
sanity long enough to shake her head. "No," she
said hoarsely. "No, I'm not married."

Twenty? Jamie had been twenty when Jimmy
was born? "Jimmy?" She sat him forward on her
lap, the better to see his face. "How old are you?"

He stared at her warily. "Nine. I'm small for my

age, but Grandpa says my dad was, too, and he grew to be over six feet."

She knew. "When is your birthday?"

"May third." He slid off her lap and curled farther back on the couch, dragging his blanket with him. "You look funny, lady. Are you gonna throw up?"

She shook her head. "No. No, I'm not." And I'm not going to faint, either, she told herself sternly. What I'm going to do is think. Try to think.

A girl. They had told her she'd had a girl. Could they have lied? They had told her she'd been stillborn. Could they have lied about that?"

No! No! This was a mistake. What she was beginning to think couldn't possibly be true! But . . . May third? Her daughter had been born on the third of May. At 2:37 in the morning. She hadn't heard her baby cry. She hadn't seen her baby's face. She had been unconscious, anesthetized. She pressed her hand to the scar on her abdomen.

"It will heal," they had told her. "In a year or two it won't even show. A bikini incision is good that way. You were having too much difficulty, dear. It was for your own good, for your baby's sake too. But . . ." There had been genuine sadness on the faces around her. "But it was too late for your little girl. She died, dear, before we got to her."

Donna had wondered then at the cruelty disguised as kindness in telling a young woman that her baby had been stillborn. Wouldn't it have been better to let her believe the child lived somewhere in a wonderful, happy home, complete with two parents, siblings maybe, grandparents and loving aunts and uncles?

No, they had said. Because she had become so unsure about adoption the closer her time came, they had been forced to tell her. "Because you cared so much. This way, my dear, knowing the truth, you can go on from here and not look back. Not be forever wondering, looking at little girls and asking yourself, 'Is this the one?' This way, you can forget this stage in your life and go on, contented, into the next."

No, she hadn't looked at little girls and wondered if that were the one. But she hadn't forgotten, either, or been content.

Now the scar on her abdomen sent a shaft of pain through her body, and she groaned aloud.

"Lady? I can't remember your name. What's wrong with you? You're hurting my hand!"

"I'm . . . What? Your hand? I'm sorry. Oh, God, Jimmy, I'm sorry. I—"

She stood and reeled to the far side of the room, where a mirror hung on the wall. She gazed at herself, then turned and looked at the boy on the sofa. It was there. Of course it was there. She wondered why she hadn't seen it at once. It was in the eyes especially. Those big brown eyes, the shape of them, the way they were set into his face at a slight angle and were surrounded by thick, dark lashes. She saw them every day in the mirror, but she'd seen them so many times, she didn't really look at them anymore. Until now, seeing them repeated on the face of this child.

Her child.

It was there in the mouth, too, the firm, straight line of it as he gazed at her, not smiling, worried, confused by her bizarre behavior.

My child. My . . . son. Her brain tripped on the word. Making the transition from a dead daughter to a living son was not easy, but she had to do it. And she had to curb her emotions, because the one thing she did not want to do was frighten this innocent little boy. This child who had been stolen from her by means she couldn't even begin to comprehend, except that she knew money had been involved. Kincaid money.

And that was why, once he knew she was back on the island, Chester had changed his offer. Not to protect his son from her, but his grandson.

He'd wanted to make sure she never knew.

Was it the resemblance between mother and child that had made him so rabidly insistent that Jimmy stay away from the campground, that had caused him to put out rumors of shotguns and buckshot? Was he afraid Tyler and Sadie would see Jimmy and know? The thought sprang to her mind that maybe they did know, and that was what had kept them from welcoming her back into their lives until they had no choice.

With a shake of her head, she rejected the notion. Her aunt and uncle were honorable people. They would never have let her be deceived in such a way.

She remembered the first day she'd met Gray, his comment on her resemblance to someone he knew. Surely he must have figured it out by now. She felt sick, and knew she must control that too. Because of the boy. Because of Jimmy. Because of her son.

She lifted her hand and watched distantly as it trembled, then made a fist and knocked on the door to Andy's room. "Andy? Andy? Wake up." She knocked again.

"Jimmy," she said to the boy, "I have to go out for a little while. My assistant will get you something to wear, and you can sleep in the other bunk in his room. Okay?"

Jimmy looked at her questioningly. "You're not gonna make me go home?"

She shook her head. "No, honey. Not tonight."

Impulsively, she bent and kissed the top of his head, kissed her child for the very first time. "Not unless you want to." His expression said he did not want to.

After she told Andy what to do, she smiled at Jimmy and said good night. But it was not, she thought as she left, going to be a very good night at all.

At least not for the Kincaid men.

Donna didn't see either Gray or Chester as an even more frazzled looking Maggie let her in. "Where is Jimmy's room?" she asked, clearly startling and confusing the woman.

"Why . . . why, upstairs, miss, but—"

"Thank you." Donna took the stairs two at a time, ignoring the protests from below. Of course, she thought. Jimmy would be in the corner room that had been his father's, with the window that faced the campground, out of which he used to hang a yellow towel to tell Donna to join him in the treehouse.

She was right. The room was exactly as Jamie had described it all those years ago, a very fancy prison. She dragged a suitcase down from the top shelf of a large closet, then opened the bureau and began stuffing in clothing. Drawer after drawer she opened, making a quick selection. No way could she take all of it, but Jimmy would have enough before she left. She snapped the case closed and grabbed a tattered teddy from the bed, tucking it under her arm.

She had reached the doorway when loud steps thundered up the carpeted stairs and she set the case down, ready to confront Chester.

He stepped into the room and bright red color

burst across his face as the fireworks began out-side.

"What in the hell are you doing here?" he de-manded.

"Packing some clothes for my son."

He stared at her, his face livid, his chest rising and falling rapidly. "What son? If you have a son, Miss Mailer, it's news to me, and why should you take my grandson's clothing to satisfy some other child's needs?"

Donna laughed. "My son, Chester," she said, making no effort to keep her voice down, "is entitled to the things in your grandson's room. Isn't he?"

"No! Of course not! You're out of your mind. That's it. You're having a nervous breakdown. Sure you are. Come with me. There's a doctor among my guests. I'll get you a sedative and—"

"Fine. Go ahead. Call anyone you like, Chester. I wouldn't mind a witness to this conversation about my son."

"Why do you expect me to care about your son? I didn't even know you had one!"

"I had one, Chester. On May third, nine years and two months ago. And my son—Jamie's son—is your grandson, Jimmy." She made it plain she was telling, not asking.

"You stole him from me," she went on, "took him because I'd started making noises about not giving my baby up for adop—"

"No!" It was a howl of anguish. "No! How did you find out? Who told you? Graham! That fool! That soft, lily-livered, useless—" He broke off and staggered past her, clinging to a post at the foot of Jimmy's bed as his big head rocked from side to side. "I didn't know Graham knew the first thing about it. I didn't think anybody knew. And you!"

Suddenly he was shouting, throttling the bedpost as if it were her throat. "The way things were set up, you should never have known you even had a son!"

"I didn't!" she shouted back at him. "I thought I had a baby girl. And they told me she was dead. You *paid* them to do that, didn't you, Chester? And why? To prevent me ever searching in the future?"

She sobbed once, harshly, and shoved her hair off her face. Somewhere, she had lost the combs that held it back. "Oh, why do I ask? Of course it was! Who would search for a dead child?" She gulped in air and continued before he could catch his breath and start in on her again.

"Oh, it worked, Chester. It worked perfectly well! Because until tonight I didn't even suspect I had a living child. Even when I saw him, I never once suspected. And do you know where he is now, Chester?"

"I know where he is now, missy, and he's safe from the likes of you. You never wanted him! What you wanted was Jamie, and through him, my money! And when your trap failed to work, you were more than willing to give up Jamie's son."

"I wasn't! I wasn't willing! I wanted my baby! Jamie wanted our baby until you turned him against me, against our child. We were going to get married. Together, we could have looked after a child. But alone, and sixteen and with no money, how could I? But I wanted her . . . him, Chester. I did!"

He snorted derisively and thumped his fist on the dresser. "You were too young to know what you wanted, and so was my son. I had to make the decisions for both of you, or sit back and watch you ruin Jamie's life."

She wiped her face with the back of her hand, and remembered that her son had made exactly the same gesture in exactly the same way, not half an hour before. "What about me, what about my life? What about my son and my right to make the decisions that affect him?"

"You have no right to Jimmy!"

"Don't I? Don't bet on it, Chester. Now that I have him, I'm keeping him!" She spun away, snatched up the suitcase, and marched for the door. He caught her and slammed her against a wall so hard, model cars rolled off their shelves.

"What the hell do you mean?" he demanded. "Now that you have him, you're keeping him? You don't have him." But she saw a frantic element of doubt, of fear, in his eyes.

She overcame the pain in her head and faced him defiantly, thrusting off his pinioning arm. "He is at my house."

"You're lying!"

"I'm not. Lying's your department, Chester, yours and your son's. And do you know why Jimmy is sleeping in a bed in my house tonight? Because you drove him there! You were so intent on making sure I never laid eyes on him again, you sent him out to spend the night aboard your boat. He, champion swimmer that he is, swam ashore rather than stay there and get seasick."

"No!" He reeled away from her and sat down hard on the bed, his eyes never leaving her face. "I'll come and get him. I have friends here. You can't fight all of us. I have custody! My lawyer, he's here. He'll tell you. I have the legal right to my grandson!"

"Like hell you do. You couldn't have adopted him, because I never signed him away. How could I? I thought my baby was dead."

Striding forward, she laughed into his white face, took deep pleasure in his pain-filled eyes, the runnels of sweat pouring down his temples. Oh, it was good, making Chester Kincaid squirm, making him hurt.

"I'm going to take him away from you," she told him. "I'm going to steal back that which is mine."

"You can't!" he gasped. "You can't take my grandson from me. He hates you."

"Yes. He hates his mother. Because of your lies. But I'll turn that around. You watch me!"

He wiped the sweat from his brow. "You have no claim. You were willing to give him up."

"Was I? Was I really, Chester? Can you prove that? I can't say one way or the other. All I know is that as my pregnancy progressed, as I felt him moving inside me and learned to love him, I wondered. I expressed my doubts to the people at the home and began exploring ways through which I might keep my baby, raise him myself."

She stared at him. "And they were reporting back to you all along, weren't they? Even though you made Jamie swear my baby wasn't his, you knew it was, or you wouldn't have taken such an interest."

Chester didn't try to deny it. "You can't have him," he said raggedly. "Do you understand me? You cannot have him! He is mine! My blood!"

"More my blood than yours, Chester! And in case you're thinking you can continue to get away with what you've done to me, a DNA test will prove conclusively that he's mine."

Chester stared at her. His chest heaved. His

eyes closed, and he slumped. She knew he was beaten. Carrying the teddy bear and the suitcase, she walked away from him. As she left the room he said behind her, "I love him."

She turned and glanced back. "As much as I loved Jamie?"

Ten

It was another hour before Gray knocked on Donna's door. She arose from the chair she'd been sitting in, waiting for him. Him, or his father, or the law. She was prepared for any of them.

"What did you do to my father?" he asked harshly when she opened the door. "What happened between you, Donna?"

"What makes you think I did something to him?"

"Dammit, Donna, don't play games! Maggie told me how you bullied your way upstairs to my nephew's room, and then when she heard you and my father shouting at each other, she went looking for me. I got there to find you gone and my father incoherent. Now, what happened?"

He was so ready to believe she was at fault! What kind of love did that imply? "Ask him," she said, turning away.

"I told you, he's incoherent! He's been sedated. I'm asking you, Donna, and I want an answer!"

She fell back a step. "Is he . . . ill?"

The look he gave her was blistering. "Do you care?"

She shook her head, weariness, worry, and a sense of deep loss washing over her. Had she reclaimed her child, only to loose the man she loved? Or had she never had him in the first place? She wanted him to know, though, that she cared if her actions hurt him. Still she would not lie. "No," she said. "I care, but only in that his health affects you. And Jimmy."

His scathing look told her how much credence he put in that statement. "I've come for Jimmy. That was one thing I managed to get out of my father, that he was here."

She stood her ground against the wall of acrimony he kept before him and said something she hadn't planned, hadn't even considered, until faced with the prospect of waking Jimmy and telling him . . . Telling him what?

"No," she said, one hand held out before her as if to fend Gray off, though he was in no way threatening her. "You can't have him. He isn't here. I've had him . . . moved."

Gray took two paces closer, shoving her hand aside. "What? Dammit, what's the matter with you? Donna, my father is beside himself!" His voice shook. "I think he's on the verge of a stroke, because of your sudden and inexplicable greed."

"Greed?" she exclaimed.

"Yes, greed! Why else would you be trying to hold my nephew, if not to extort even more money from my father? Wasn't his offer enough? I thought it was! I thought it was damned generous. And so did you a couple of hours ago, until you got your hands on Jimmy and decided to go for the whole bundle." His nostrils flared. His mouth was a hard, taut line. "Extortion's a pretty filthy crime, Donna, right up there with a kidnapping."

She stared at him. "Kidnapping?"

"What else would you call keeping Jimmy until we come up with the money you're demanding? If you force me to, I'll have to see what the law calls it, so don't let it go that far, Donna." Suddenly, he softened toward her, touching her face with one hand. "For the love of God, don't make me put you in jail. Just give me my nephew and I'll go."

She knocked his hand away. "Are you out of your mind? If anyone should go to jail, it's your father! Jimmy came here of his own accord. He came because of your father's abuse. I didn't kidnap him. There's been no attempt at ex—"

Gray cut her off. "My father has never abused that boy! You're the one who suffers from insanity!" Pain creased his face, disbelief and confusion too. He rubbed his brow as if his head ached. "Oh, hell, Donna, do you know how hard this is for me?" He was pleading now. "I love you, and I find I can't turn it off just like that. I can hardly believe you've done this, except for the evidence of my own eyes." He kicked the suitcase she'd dropped on the floor, sending the teddy bear tumbling. "Can't you see what you're doing? Are you so completely amoral that you don't know right from wrong?"

She grabbed up the teddy and hugged it. "Your father's the amoral one. He—"

"Stop it!" he shouted. "Just stop accusing my father of things." He stared at her, his eyes hollow, his cheeks drawn. "I can see now why he was so willing to up his offer and make it worth your while to leave. You're exactly what he told me you were, greedy, selfish, out of the main chance." He laughed bitterly and brushed his hair off his forehead. "He warned me about you, you know, just this afternoon, but I chose not to believe him. On a personal level, I couldn't believe him. Not only had I fallen in love with you, but I liked you, admired you because you gave up a life and a home you claimed to love, to come here and care for your aunt and uncle. I thought that made you the kind of compassionate, caring woman I could love for the rest of my life. The sexual attraction was just a bonus."

"Fallen in love with me?" she repeated. "Hah!" Her voice cracked. "You had no more fallen in love with me than your father had. What you were trying desperately to do was follow his orders and get me to sell out before I came back and discovered Jimmy!"

"We've managed to protect Jimmy from kidnappers this far. Why should we have worried especially about you?"

"Damn you! Damn you, Gray!" Tossing the bear onto the couch, she flew at him, beating him with her fists, trying to kick him, her fury overwhelming her as she wept and shouted. "Will you stop calling me a kidnapper? If there are any charges of kidnapping to be laid here, I'll be the one laying them—against your father!"

"What the hell are you talking about?" he bellowed. "I've had enough of this. Either you produce my nephew so I can take him home to my father, or you'll be dealing with the Mounties before morning."

"No. No. No." She shook her head determinedly with each utterance of the word. "Don't ask me to give him up, Gray. I can't do it. I can't. Oh, please, why don't you believe me? I'm telling you the truth!" She sank onto a chair and buried her face in her hands. "Just once, just once in my life, I wanted to win over Chester Kincaid. Why can't you love me enough to believe me?"

"Donna . . ." Her tears, her wracking sobs, undid him. He crouched before her and ran his hands up her arms. "Sweetheart, listen to me. I don't know what this vendetta is you have against my father, but you can't go on doing this. I promised my father I'd bring Jimmy back to him. Have a little pity for an old man, please, and for a little boy who loves his grandfather. How will you explain it to Jimmy, when he wakes up in the morning and wants to go home, and you have to tell him he can't?"

"He can't, he can't," she wept. "Oh, Gray, he has to stay with me."

"Love, don't force me to use violence to take the child from you simply because you hate my father."

"Use violence?" Donna could stand no more. She leaped up and flung herself past him. He made no move to stop her, only came slowly erect, pulling himself up, his eyes dark and pain-filled. "The way violence was used to take him from me in the beginning, you mean?"

He stared at her uncomprehending. "Take him from you? In the beginning? Beginning of what? What the hell are you talking about?"

"Oh, what an act!" she said. "You do it well, Graham Kincaid! If I didn't know better, I'd think you really didn't know what they did to me."

"I don't. What who did to you? When?" He shook his head. "None of what you're saying makes sense, Donna."

"Doesn't it? All right, granted, you may never have been told how they did it, though you know full well what they did. Maybe even your father and brother would have been too ashamed to tell you all the details.

"They—the staff at the home—told me my labor was threatening my life, and I was young, stupid, and alone. How did I know if it was true or not? They said I might die, and so might my baby, if they didn't operate to take her."

She began crying, distraught, begging for his understanding. "I wanted my baby to live, Gray. I wanted her so much! I had no one, you see, no one of my own, because my parents were dead and my aunt and uncle were ashamed of me and Jamie had betrayed me, so I told them to go ahead, to do what they had to do to save my baby, to give me a baby to love, someone—someone all my own. Then they . . . put me under, and when I woke up, they said my little girl had died. I didn't know it wasn't true. Not until today. Oh, Gray, please, please understand! I didn't know until tonight when Jimmy came here and told me who he was, that they had cut me open and stolen my baby, then lied to me when they told me she had died!"

He stared at her as if she'd started speaking in tongues. "Donna, for the love of God! Are you out of your mind?" He grabbed her again, holding her before him, staring fiercely at her. "Donna, sweetheart . . .You had a baby once, is that it? And she died, and for some reason, you're blaming my father?"

She shook herself free of his grasp. "I'm blaming your father for the simple reason that he is to blame! He stole my baby! You think that's not an act of violence? Jimmy is my child, Gray! Believe me, I'm not crazy. I'm not imagining things. He's mine!"

"What do you mean, I'm yours?"

Gray and Donna both whirled at the sound of

the hoarse young voice. Jimmy stared at them, his brown eyes huge, his face white, anger pulsating from him. He shoved up the sleeves of the sweat-shirt Andy had found for him to wear, and his clenched fists made taut, corded muscle ridges along his forearms. His young face looked fright-eningly old.

"Yours?" he said again incredulously. "*You're* my mother?" Then, in a blast of repudiation, he yelled, "No! Forget it, lady! I don't want a mother! I don't need a mother! I don't need you!"

"Jimmy . . ." Donna's voice was a moan of pain deeper than any pain Gray had heard before. His gaze swept from his nephew's set face to the face of the woman he loved, and he instantly saw the similarities he should have seen—had seen, but failed to recognize—before.

He slumped against the table. "Oh, my God," he said slowly. "Oh, dear God! Now what?"

As if he had heard the truth in his uncle's voice, Jimmy appealed to him. "Uncle Graham? It isn't true, is it? She's not really my mother?"

Gray stood very still for several long moments, making the comparisons he knew he must have been blind to miss. His throat ached with the bellow of denial he wanted to make as he thought of Donna . . . and Jamie . . . and wrestled with the reality he had to face. With utmost difficulty, he nodded.

"Yes," he said in a rough whisper. "Yes, Jimmy. She really is."

"*Why?*"

If Donna's moan had expressed agony, this cry, coming from a small child, told of unspeakable torture. Jimmy backed up against the wall, star-ing at Donna with horror, with hate. "You left me!"

he accused. "You didn't want me! I hate you, you lousy, filthy bi—"

"Jimmy!" Gray's voice thundered into the room cutting through the child's outburst.

"No." Donna stepped between them. "Leave him alone, Gray. He's entitled to what he feels."

"He's not entitled to call you names."

She gave him a bleak look. "Why not? Haven't you been, in your mind, ever since I started to tell you? Ever since you took your father's part against me? Why don't you go, Gray? Leave us alone, my son and me. We have things to sort out. I'm sure Jimmy has things he wants to ask me."

Jimmy picked up his teddy bear, which he seemed not at all surprised to find on the couch. He kept his gaze on her face, resentful, angry. "Yeah," he said. "Damn right. I got lots to ask you, lady."

His hostility was like a shield he held between them, fending off any move she might make in his direction. It should have been ludicrous, she thought, the small, brown-eyed child standing there clutching his teddy bear and staring at her with more venom than she'd ever experienced, even from Chester Kincaid, but it was not. It was tragic. There were no fairy-tale endings about to happen here, Donna could see. Her son wasn't going to leap across the room into her arms, full of loving forgiveness simply because she was his mother. If he ever learned to like her, to trust her, it was going to take a lot of giving on her part, a lot of healing on his, and she wasn't even sure he wanted to heal. Maybe, like his grandfather, he found it easier to hate women. Could misogyny be inherited, or was it simply learned? Wherever it came from, James Alexander Kincaid had a severe case, one she thought might never be cured.

She steeled herself and said, "Go ahead, Jimmy. I'll answer any question you want to ask."

His first one came as a complete surprise. "Do I gotta call you Mom?"

She winced as she sank down onto a kitchen chair. "No, of course not. My name is Donna. That's what you can call me." *Mama*, she thought. *Mommy. Mom. Who do I ache to hear those words? I never did before. Not like this. Not this bad!*

Jimmy maintained his belligerent stance. "How come you didn't want me?"

She heard Gray draw a sharp breath and gestured for him to be still. It appeared he had no intention of leaving, as she'd asked him to.

"I did want you," she said. "There was a . . . mistake. A mix-up, and I lost you, but I wanted you then and I want you now. I always will."

His eyes widened, not with pleasure. "Does that mean I gotta live with you?"

"No," she said quickly. "Not unless you choose to. I won't take you away from your grandpa. I know you love him. But I would like to have you spend some time with me, so we can get to know each other properly."

"Like when you're not on tours and stuff, huh?"

"Tours?"

"You know. Like rock groups. Are you a star? I've never seen you on TV."

She shook her head. "No. I've never been a singer of any kind." She found a smile somewhere within her pain and gave it to him. All she'd ever given him before was hot chocolate and a bandage. She could at least smile for him. "I never wanted to be. And I don't go on tours. I plan to live right here so you can come and visit me anytime you want."

He frowned. "How come you went away, then, if you're not a singer?"

"Jimmy, will you sit down, please? I think we have a lot to talk about, and we may as well be comfortable." She pushed out another chair at the table, but he was too wary. He perched on the sofa, separated from her by the table and six feet of floor, still clutching his teddy bear.

Fair enough, she thought. He had absolutely no reason to trust her. That was something she was going to have to earn.

"I went away, Jimmy, because I was sixteen years old and pregnant and that was what I was told to do. I had no choice in the matter. My uncle and aunt, and your grandpa, made the decision. Maybe if I'd been a little bit older, I would have fought them on it, but I wasn't and I didn't. I'm sorry about that now."

"Did you want to have a baby, or did you just get pregnant so you could get my grandpa's money?"

She hesitated only briefly. One other thing she could give this child of hers was the truth about why he'd been conceived. "I wanted to have a baby," she said. "If your grandfather told you I set out to get pregnant, then he was right. I did. I knew about birth control. We both did, your father and I, but we chose to have a baby together. We wanted to have someone of our very own, you see, because we were both lonely people and we didn't want to be lonely anymore. We weren't very smart, as it turns out, because having a baby to make you not feel lonely is one of the worst reasons ever."

He chewed on that for a while. "How come?"

"A baby should be born because its parents want to do something wonderful for another human being, like giving him a chance to live and a happy, secure place to do it. What your father and I did was selfish and foolish and childish, because we had no guarantees that we could give you a happy, secure place to live. All we had was a dream and a hope, and we soon found out that we were too young, and too powerless, to make our own dreams come true."

"So you gave me away." His face was puzzled. "But my grandpa found me? Where? How?"

She sighed. "I know you don't understand, Jimmy. It's hard for me to understand, too, but we have to try. Your grandpa believed that I didn't want you, that I was going to let some other people adopt you." She met his gaze squarely. "That might have happened too. I don't know what I would have done in the end."

She smiled again. "It was what had been planned for me all along, you see, by the people who were looking after me. It's what a lot of girls do when they can't look after their babies themselves. And, I believe, it would have been the right thing for you, to have a mom and dad and maybe some brothers and sisters."

"So how come you didn't do that?"

"Because there was a . . . mistake. Somebody must have gotten you and me mixed up with some other baby and his mother, and they told me you had died. So of course I didn't sign any adoption papers. I went and got a job in a place far away from where you were born. Then, I guess, when they found out the mistake had been made, they couldn't find me and got in touch with your dad and your grandparents. They came and got you, because they loved you too."

He looked troubled as he rubbed his bear's ear between his finger and thumb.

"If they loved me," he asked, "why did they make

you go away to have me? Why didn't my dad marry you and then you and him could have been my mom and dad together and none of this would ever have happened?"

"Jimmy . . ." Distressed, she searched for the right words. "Your grandpa loved your dad very much. He wanted what he thought was best for him. And my aunt and uncle loved me, too, and were sure I was too young to be a wife and a mom. They were probably right. All of them. But it's too late to know, isn't it? Things happened the way they did, whether they were right or wrong. What we can do now is try to make something good and happy out of what we have."

He yawned and leaned back. "I guess." He glanced up at her. "Are you happy you got a son?"

"I sure am."

"I'd feel kinda funny, callin' you Mom."

"I know, honey. It's all right. I told you, you can call me Donna."

"Okay. Can I go back to bed now, Donna?"

"Sure. May I tuck you in?"

He shrugged. "I s'pose."

It was only then that Donna noticed Gray had left, and she hadn't even seen him go.

He returned to the campground the following morning, with his father. Donna stood on the front porch, watching them alight from Gray's car, and walk slowly, arm in arm, up onto the porch. Then she felt the breeze as Jimmy dashed by her and flung himself into his grandfather's arms. Gray stood well apart from her, his eyes, like hers, on the reunion between the old man and the little boy.

"I swam ashore, Grandpa! In the night! It was

cold and scary but I was awful seasick and Mack wouldn't radio you for permission to bring me back. Are you mad at me?"

Chester scooped Jimmy up and held him close. "No, son. I'm not mad at you." He tipped Jimmy back in his arms. "Hey, I hear you've found yourself a mom. How do you feel about that?"

Jimmy smiled and shrugged one skinny shoulder. "Pretty good, I think. You know, she never was a singer and she thought I was dead. That's why she went away and they couldn't find her. She says it was lucky for me that the hospital people knew how to find you, so at least I could grow up having a grandpa."

"And a father and an uncle," Chester reminded him. Donna noticed the absense of any mention of a grandmother. "And speaking of your uncle, how'd you like to take a walk with him, so I can have a private talk with Miss . . . with your mother?"

Gray finally looked at Donna, a question in his eyes.

She nodded, and Chester set Jimmy on his feet.

They watched as Jimmy and Gray walked away, heading for, Donna guessed, the treehouse. She invited Chester inside, but he declined, perching instead on the swing.

"First," he said, "I want to apologize, though I know it's years too late and too much has happened to you, too many bad things, for you ever to forgive." He looked up at her, for she had remained standing, and met her gaze. "But I want you to know I'm sorry for what I did."

"Why?" she asked. "Because you got caught?"

He winced, and for the first time she saw a resemblance to Gray in his face. "I deserved that. Will you at least let me explain?"

After a moment she nodded and leaned back

against the porch rail. Chester talked for nearly half an hour, about Jamie and Jimmy, about why he had wanted his grandson so much. At last, he stood. "I'll go now," he said, "and send my son back to you." He smiled faintly. "What is it about you that makes my sons love you? Maybe this time you'll stay around long enough that I'll find out, hmm?"

Donna didn't reply. Someday, she might forgive Chester. As for how long she'd stay around, that depended on several factors she didn't think she could control.

"Hi."

Donna turned from where she sat on the porch rail, her feet dangling. She couldn't speak, could do nothing more than nod her head once and tug the sash of her robe as if it were about to come undone, the way she felt she was coming undone. She told herself that no matter what, she would not cry. Even if he said it was all over because she hadn't been as open with him as he'd been with her, and he didn't like a woman who held back the important things, like a long-ago affair with a man's own brother."

"Could . . ." Gray cleared his throat. "Could we talk?"

"What about?"

"Us."

The tears she had forsworn stung the back of her eyes. "Is there an 'us'?" The fear she couldn't contain tinged her voice.

He smiled. "I love you. If you love me only half as much, then yes, there is an 'us.'"

"I didn't tell you about Jamie and me. I should have."

"And I'm sure you would have. When you felt you trusted me enough."

She closed her eyes for a moment and clung to the rail as tightly as she could. "What about Trish?"

He waited until she met his gaze. "What about my father?" he countered. "What about Jimmy? Are they going to interfere with our relationship?"

"I want Jimmy to live with me. I believe he will, someday. If not, then I'll want to stay here, close."

"That suits me. I think that together, you and I could turn this place around and make it the kind of paying proposition your uncle once ran."

She stared at him. "What about your job?"

"I told you, I quit."

He sat on the swing, his head bowed, his hands linked between his knees. "I'm so ashamed, Donna," he said softly. "And you know the funny part of it? When I heard the whole story, when I knew the depths my father had sunk to and learned what a gutless little coward my brother turned out to be, my first instinct was to take you away, to protect you and hide you from the obscenity of the Kincaid family. But then I realized that I was the last man on earth who could do that. Because I'm one of them."

He looked up, and she saw the glint of tears in his silver eyes.

"I thought I was ashamed of my father before," he went on, "but after learning what he did to you—and to Jimmy—I feel sick to death. I wish I could walk away and never see him again. But . . ." His mouth twisted.

"But he's your father," she said tenderly. "You love him. That's okay with me, Gray. I wouldn't love a man who couldn't forgive sins. Even big ones."

He stood and looked straight at her, not wavering. "Like I said once before, you're a very classy lady."

"Forgive him, Gray. You have to do that for your own sake."

He wrapped his hands around her shoulders. "Have you forgiven him?"

She didn't reply for a moment. "I don't know," she said. "I'd like to. He told me he took Jimmy because he knew he'd made a hash of raising Jamie, and he wanted another chance." She smiled. "And apart from that particularly foul tongue my son has, I think he's succeeded so far. At least Jimmy has some intestinal fortitude."

Gray lifted her off the rail. "He sure does." He smiled again. "But I think that's something he inherited directly down the maternal line. You know, it's so strange that you never asked me whose child Jimmy was. If I'd thought you didn't know, I'd have told you out there by the treehouse yesterday."

"I didn't ask because there was never much of an opportunity, and I assumed he belonged to one of your stepbrothers or sisters. I thought you'd brought him along as a playmate for Trish."

"Trish." He shook his head. "What a kid. When I told her about you and me, she said, 'Wow! It's about time, Daddy. You really aren't the best cook in the world, you know.' Then she thought about it for a few more minutes and said, 'When I like Jimmy, I can tell people he's my cousin. When I don't, I can say he's just my stepbrother and there's nothing I can do about it.'"

Donna spluttered with laughter. "You know," she said several moments later, "I never realized before I met you that a person could smooch and laugh at the same time."

He rocked her back and forth, smooching and laughing. His hands slid over the curves of her shoulders, drawing her closer. "I think the rest of this discussion would be better held indoors," he said huskily. "Because there are things I can say easier without words."

"What things?" she asked, as the door swung shut behind them.

"This, for one." He pulled her tightly against him, sliding one hand up into her hair and tilting her head back. He kissed her, long and deeply and thoroughly. When he lifted his head, he looked as dazed as she felt. "I love you," he said. His eyes probed hers, demanding an answer.

Unable to hold her tears back any longer, she dropped her forehead to his chest. With her arms wrapped around him, she could feel his rapid breathing, his trip-hammer heartbeat. "Oh, Gray, if you didn't love me, I'd die."

"I want to spend the rest of my life with you," he said, "because there are a lot of things *I* never realized before I met *you*."

"Like what?"

"Well, for one, that it's possible for a man to be horny twenty-four hours a day after the age of eighteen."

"Oh," she managed to say before he kissed her again.

"Donna? Sweetheart?"

"Mmm?" Reluctantly, she opened her eyes and looked at him.

"You haven't given me an answer yet. Will you marry me?"

Head tilted coyly, she answered his question with one of her own. "How long past the age of eighteen?"

THE EDITOR'S CORNER

What could be more romantic than weddings? Picture the bride in an exquisite gown. Imagine the handsome groom in a finely tailored tuxedo. Hear them promise "to have and to hold" each other forever. This is the perfect ending to courtship, the joyous ritual we cherish in our hearts. And next month, in honor of June brides, we present six fabulous LOVESWEPTs with beautiful brides and handsome grooms on the covers.

Leading the line-up is **HER VERY OWN BUTLER,** LOVESWEPT #552, another sure-to-please romance from Helen Mittermeyer. Single mom Drew Laughlin wanted a butler to help run her household, but she never expected a muscled, bronzed Hercules to apply. Rex Dakeland promised an old friend to check up on Drew and her children, but keeping his secret soon feels too much like spying. Once unexpected love ensnares them both, could he win her trust and be her one and only? A real treat, from one of romance's best-loved authors.

Gail Douglas pulls out all the stops in **ALL THE WAY,** LOVESWEPT #553. Jake Mallory and Brittany Thomas shared one fabulous night together, but he couldn't convince her it was enough to build their future on. Now, six months later, Jake is back from his restless wandering and sets out to prove to Brittany that he's right. It'll take fiery kisses and spellbinding charm to make her believe that the reckless nomad is finally ready to put down roots. Gail will win you over with this charming love story.

WHERE THERE'S A WILL . . . by Victoria Leigh, LOVESWEPT #554, is a sheer delight. Maggie Cooper plays a ditzy seductress on the ski slopes, only to prove to herself that she's sexy enough to kindle a man's desire. And boy, does she kindle Will Jackson's desire! He usually likes to do the hunting, but letting Maggie work her wiles on him is tantalizing fun. And after he's freed her from her doubts, he'll teach her to dare to love. There's a lot of wonderful verve and dash in this romance from talented Victoria.

Laura Taylor presents a very moving, very emotional love story in **DESERT ROSE**, LOVESWEPT #555. Emma Hamilton and David Winslow are strangers caught in a desperate situation, wrongfully imprisoned in a foreign country. Locked in adjacent cells, they whisper comfort to each other and reach through iron bars to touch hands. Love blossoms between them in that dark prison, a love strong enough to survive until fate finally brings them freedom. You'll cry and cheer for these memorable lovers. Bravo, Laura!

There's no better way to describe Deacon Brody than **RASCAL,** Charlotte Hughes's new LOVESWEPT, #556. He was once a country-music sensation, and he's never forgotten how hard he struggled to make it—or the woman who broke his heart. Losing Cody Sherwood sends him to Nashville determined to make her sorry she let him go, but when he sees her again, he realizes he's never stopped wanting her or the passion that burned so sweetly between them. Charlotte delivers this story with force and fire.

Please give a rousing welcome to Bonnie Pega and her first novel, **ONLY YOU,** LOVESWEPT #557. To efficiency expert Max Shore, organizing Caitlin Love's messy office is a snap compared to uncovering the sensual woman beneath her professional facade. A past pain has etched caution deep in her heart, and only Max can show her how to love again. This enchanting novel will show you why we're excited to have Bonnie writing for LOVESWEPT. Enjoy one of our New Faces of '92!

On sale this month from FANFARE are three marvelous novels. The historical romance **HEATHER AND VELVET** showcases the exciting talent of a rising star—Teresa Medeiros. Her marvelous touch for creating memorable characters and her exquisite feel for portraying passion and emotion shine in this grand adventure of love between a bookish orphan and a notorious highwayman known as the Dreadful Scot Bandit. Ranging from the storm-swept English countryside to the wild moors of Scotland, **HEATHER AND VELVET** has garnered the following praise from *New York Times* bestselling author Amanda Quick: "A terrific tale full of larger-than-life characters and thrilling romance." Teresa Medeiros—a name to watch for.

Lush, dramatic, and poignant, **LADY HELLFIRE** by Suzanne Robinson is an immensely thrilling historical romance. Its hero, Alexis de Granville, Marquess of Richfield, is a cold-blooded rogue whose tragic—and possibly violent—past has hardened his heart to love . . . until he melts at the fiery touch of Kate Grey's sensual embrace.

Anna Eberhardt, who writes short romances under the pseudonym Tiffany White, has been nominated for *Romantic Times*'s Career Achievement award for Most Sensual Romance in a series. In **WHISPERED HEAT**, she delivers a compelling contemporary novel of love lost, then regained. When Slader Reems is freed after five years of being wrongly imprisoned, he sets out to reclaim everything that was taken from him—including Lissa Jamison.

Also on sale this month, in the Doubleday hardcover edition, is **HIGHLAND FLAME** by Stephanie Bartlett, the stand-alone "sequel" to **HIGHLAND REBEL**. Catriona Galbaith, now a widow, is thrust into a new struggle—and the arms of a new love.

Happy reading!

With best wishes,

Nita Taublib

Nita Taublib
Associate Publisher
LOVESWEPT and FANFARE

FANFARE

On Sale in May

HEATHER AND VELVET

☐ 29407-5 $4.99/5.99 in Canada
by Teresa Medeiros

She was an innocent lass who haunted a highwayman's dreams.
"A terrific tale full of larger-than-life characters and
thrilling romance."
--Amanda Quick, New York Times bestselling author

LADY HELLFIRE

☐ 29678-7 $4.99/5.99 in Canada
by Suzanne Robinson

author of LADY GALLANT

A rakehell English lord . . . A brazen Yankee heiress . . .
And a passion that would set their hearts aflame . . .
"Excellent reading." --Rendezvous

WHISPERED HEAT

☐ 29608-6 $4.99/5.99 in Canada
by Anna Eberhardt

A sizzling contemporary romance.
"Sensual . . . sexy . . . a treat to read."
--Sandra Brown, New York Times bestselling author

THE SYMBOL OF GREAT WOMEN'S FICTION FROM BANTAM

Ask for these books at your local bookstore or use this page to order.

FANFARE

FANFARE

Rosanne Bittner

_____ 28599-8 EMBERS OF THE HEART . $4.50/5.50 in Canada

_____ 29033-9 IN THE SHADOW OF THE MOUNTAINS
$5.50/6.99 in Canada

_____ 28319-7 MONTANA WOMAN .... $4.50/5.50 in Canada

_____ 29014-2 SONG OF THE WOLF .... $4.99/5.99 in Canada

Deborah Smith

_____ 28759-1 THE BELOVED WOMAN .. $4.50/ 5.50 in Canada

_____ 29092-4 FOLLOW THE SUN .... $4.99/ 5.99 in Canada

_____ 29107-6 MIRACLE .... $4.50/ 5.50 in Canada

Tami Hoag

_____ 29053-3 MAGIC .... $3.99/4.99 in Canada

Dianne Edouard and Sandra Ware

_____ 28929-2 MORTAL SINS .... $4.99/5.99 in Canada

Kay Hooper

_____ 29256-0 THE MATCHMAKER, ... $4.50/5.50 in Canada

_____ 28953-5 STAR-CROSSED LOVERS .. $4.50/5.50 in Canada

Virginia Lynn

_____ 29257-9 CUTTER'S WOMAN, ... $4.50/4.50 in Canada

_____ 28622-6 RIVER'S DREAM, ... $3.95/4.95 in Canada

Patricia Potter

_____ 29071-1 LAWLESS .... $4.99/ 5.99 in Canada

_____ 29069-X RAINBOW .... $4.99/ 5.99 in Canada